J  2.95

# DESERT STAKE-OUT

Blade Merrick followed the sound of the distant gunfire and the scream of Apaches. The sight that greeted him was three hardcases near the charred wagon, waiting, watching. And the woman, her face distorted by fear. Fear of the Apaches? Blake looked at the men. Maybe not.

*Books by Harry Whittington*
*in the Linford Western Library:*

**TROUBLE RIDES TALL**
**HIGH FURY**
**SADDLE THE STORM**

# HARRY WHITINGTON

◆

# DESERT STAKE-OUT

*Complete and Unabridged*

## LINFORD
*Leicester*

First published in the
United States of America in 1961 by
Fawcett Publications Inc., Greenwich, Conn.

First Linford Edition
published December 1990

British Library CIP Data

Whittington, Harry, *1915–*
Desert stake-out.– Large print ed.–
Linford western library
I. Title
813.52[F]

ISBN 0–7089–6947–X

Published by
F. A. Thorpe (Publishing) Ltd.
Anstey, Leicestershire

Set by Words & Graphics Ltd.
Anstey, Leicestershire
Printed and bound in Great Britain by
T. J. Press (Padstow) Ltd., Padstow, Cornwall

To Harry Joe Brown

# 1

LESS than a mile from the water hole were the bleached bones of a horse. They remained, ash-white and petrified, no longer yielding up anything to the pitiless sun. If the horse had had a rider, there was no trace of him, no memory. There was only the water hole, hidden, secret — named Patchee Wells by the few men who knew, had heard or dreamed frantically of it as throat tightened, tongue swelled. It was the only water within forty miles in a forsaken, rectilinear area of parched waste.

For days, sometimes for weeks, the water hole lay silent with its terrible, infinite stillness. A buzzard traced a high arc in the cloudless sky. A coyote sniffed, trembling; it drank, darted into the mesquite and greasewood, lost. A sidewinder slid through the rocks, and the water made a cool sound, spilling on a worn stone, and the stillness was magnified by the soft cool whisper of the water.

Stretching away from the rock-walled sump all the way to the heat-shimmering horizon lay flat gray alkali and sage wastes. Beyond, the hills were as dry as the flats, burned, shunned. In the mountains, three days' ride, were water and grass and shade, but between, the badlands lay like hot spikes, reflecting the brass of the sun.

Infrequently, a white man or a roving band of Indians came to the water hole that was a living thing upon this warped and festered scab of earth, calling to a man like the faint, tormenting whisper of a bawd. But the man passed, and the Indians; the silence settled again, breathless and unbroken.

Only the water hole remained forever.

For an hour now he had felt the brassy bite of his old chest scar and he rubbed at it with the back of his hand. Watchful, tense, he had not yet seen or heard anything, but the itch of that scar told him as plainly as though someone had spoken the words, 'Apache trouble.'

He glanced over his shoulder but did not speed the ponderous gait of the two army dray horses. He recognized that upon this limitless playa, the army wagon and himself, alone on its boot, were the only movement, and were almost lost in the gray land of heat and silence.

He was a day and a half south of Fort Ambush, still two days north of the mission at San Carlos. *The Apache strikes first and asks questions later, and that puts me in a bad spot,* he thought, and then he loosed another button of his gray shirt and mopped at his face with a bandana, thinking, *A bad spot, that's about the story of my life.*

Ahead of him was a rise, stubbled with mesquite and rock, and beyond the rise, the land fell away into a tree-less valley. Behind him were a few stunted piñon and more boulders, offering as much danger as concealment. He figured ahead the hours to Patchee Wells. No way to

3

escape trouble there, but at least a man could get a cold drink of water.

He touched the rifle on the boot beside him, glanced once more around the gray canvas wagon covering. He grinned faintly. The trouble wasn't behind him; it was ahead. When there was trouble, he was always riding into it, not away from it.

He felt a faint rise of anger that he'd allowed himself to be pushed into a position like this where he could not even run, couldn't even put his back against a wall. He'd had enough trouble with the Apache to last him a lifetime. It had been six years now, but he remembered that trouble, relived it in nightmares two and three times week. He thought about it now, and even thinking about it was a torment. He mopped his sweated face again, thinking about cold water for himself and the horses, just out of reach ahead there at Patchee Wells.

He was a tall man, lean in the belly, wide in the shoulders, with hair faded by desert suns, eyes bleached blue and shadowed with old hurts. Tragedy drew bitter lines about his eyes and mouth, so even when he smiled it was an acid caricature of a smile. There was about him the kind of wariness that grows in a man who lives alone and stays alive by being alert to everything, the crying scold of a jaybird, the whisper of wind in a pine, the clatter of a small stone on a hillside.

He was almost to the top of the knoll. The midmorning silence was broken by distant gunfire, the scream of Apaches. He rubbed at his chest with the back of his hand. He'd been right all the time. The trouble was ahead of him.

A day and a half ago in Major Ralph Brackett's quarters at Fort Ambush, he'd wanted to say no, and it seemed to him the Major had read his mind and talked fast so he didn't have a chance to say anything.

"Sure, Blade, I could send a cavalry company," the Major said, answering the question that had been bothering

5

Merrick. "You ask why I don't send a cavalry company — "

"I'd like to ask it, if I got a chance to ask anything."

"Its a good question." Major Brackett's voice increased in speed. "Its the surest way I know to guarantee those supplies would never get to the mission at San Carlos." He strode about the room. "Now, Blade, you and I are old hands out here. We respect the Apache. No company in this fort could stand up against a dozen Apaches in their own backyard and you know it."

Blade Merrick gave the Major one of his bitter smiles. "I know if the Confederacy had had a few troops of Mescaleros, that war wouldn't be over yet."

The Major stood with his back to Merrick. He stared out the window at the red parade grounds where a company marched in the sun.

"Merrick, it's an epidemic at San Carlos. I won't minimize the terror those people are going through. Fever.

6

They have doctors, a couple of them, and the nuns at the mission are doing the nursing. They don't ask me for doctors or nurses. All they want are drugs and medical supplies. The need is urgent. I haven't slept, trying to figure it. Suddenly this morning, you ride into the fort, and the whole answer comes to me. You could take a wagon of supplies down there to the mission at San Carlos. Blade Merrick. I almost laughed aloud because the whole thing was so simple. I've already ordered the wagon loaded. You can get out of here inside an hour."

"That's just fine," Blade said. "And what are you going to do when I start out of here with a wagon of medical supplies all by myself?"

"Well, first thing I'm going to do is hit the sack and get some sleep. Man, I been up all night."

Hardhead Charley Clinton stood up cautiously when the six redskin raiders suddenly jerked the heads of their ponies

7

around and raced toward the hills west at the mouth of this valley.

He cursed, forgetting the woman crouched near him. But he would have cursed if he'd remembered her. This was no time to think about social niceties, and oaths were the major part of his vocabulary. And what else was there to do but curse helplessly at the fate that had put him down here at this moment — four dead horses, a burning wagon, a wounded man, a woman, and a thousand square miles of hostile land, hot and dry and endless? Perch and young Billy were unhurt, but with dead horses they were as helpless as he was.

He was a big man, standing with legs apart, his hat knocked off during the attack and forgotten. Hardhead Charley had Nordic ancestors. He looked like a Viking pirate.

His hand tightened on his rifle. He had blue eyes with a squinted, snow-blind look to them. He had the twisted mouth, the scraggly beard of the blond Viking. He had been placed in the desert country by some whim of addled fate, out of time, out of place.

He cursed at the top of his bass voice, hurling curses after the plume of dust. He always talked loudly, accustomed to the wild places where wind dashed a timid man's voice to atoms. And a man had to be heard to be obeyed. Hardhead Charley Clinton intended to be obeyed when he spoke. A man must be obeyed, to be a man.

He drew in a breath through distended nostrils and his pirate face twisted into a scowl.

He heeled around, staring at the burning wagon, reduced now almost to charred ashes. The Indians were gone and they were going to return, five people afoot in these wastes. Him, with riches in his grasp, and no chance to get out of this bind alive. Suddenly, the matter that offended Hardhead Charley the most was the burning stench from the body of that overturned wagon.

"Name of God, woman, what in goodbilly hell you toting in that wagon to stink thataway?"

Valerie Butler cradled Jeff's head in her lap and stared up at the loud, foul-mouthed man. He looked to her to be about fifty, but it didn't seem possible a man could become so evil-tongued in only half a century.

"I don't know what it is," she answered him. Her red hair trembled about her shoulders and her green eyes impaled him. "Why don't you go look and see?"

Hardly knowing what she did, she soothed Jeff's brow with her smoke-blackened hands. All she knew was that everything she owned was in that wagon, burned now to ashes. And she had to endure sarcasm from that rotten old man.

"Let the little lady alone, Hardhead Charley," Perch Fisher said.

Hardhead glanced around at Perch, thinking that every day Perch got a little smarter, a little harder to handle. He thought about settling the matter right now. A man like Perch, you had to show him; every once in a while you

10

had to show him that you were the boss and that Perch was taking orders. He wanted to put Perch in his place, relieve some of his anger and rage at being left afoot in this waste by chewing Perch out so bad he rocked on his heels. But at the moment, Perch's stepping out of line didn't seem to pull much leather.

Perch slapped around his pockets, seeking a cigarette, his face pulled crooked with a contemptuous smile. Old Man Clinton better not push it, not in this heat, not after what they'd been through, not in front of this woman.

Perch turned his back on Hardhead Charley, looking the woman over again. Hot damn. He'd thought that the first time he saw her on the trail this morning. He still thought that. Hot smoking damn. This was the kind of woman a man walked barefoot through broken glass for. A man didn't meet her kind every day, not even in the hook-joints at Laredo. She was in her early twenties, tall and lush. Even with her hair loose on her shoulders, her face streaked with soot, a blue welt along the squared planes of her jaw, it was plain a man called her a lady — but she knew better, too.

She was in a state of shock, that was clear enough. But she wasn't so far gone she couldn't hand back to old Hardhead Charley better than he could give her.

Perch looked at the wounded man stretched out with his head in the woman's lap. It hadn't taken them long to learn today there wasn't much to her husband. It took an Indian bullet to shut him up. He had leaked a lot of blood, but the woman wasn't looking at it, as if as long as she didn't see it, she wouldn't have to believe her husband was dying with a bullet in his belly.

"Anything I can do for you, ma'am?" Perch said. He'd found a cigarette he'd rolled while waiting for the Apaches to come into rifle range this morning. He thumbed fire from a sulphur match and lighted up, watching her through a curl of smoke.

"He's dying," she said. Her voice was low, flat.

"Yes, ma'am, looks like he is." Perch gave her a rancid smile. He would have liked to look unhappy, but, seemed to him, a thing like this called for a drink. Slightly taller than Hardhead Charley, Perch Fisher weighed two hundred pounds, and pain never bothered him, certainly not another man's pain.

He batted dust from his blue trousers and black vest. He took off his flat-brimmed hat, inspected a bullet-rent in its crown.

"Man out here," he said, "chances dying every day. It ain't good for a lady like you to think about, but that's the way it is."

Young Billy Clinton emitted a fluted laugh. He sat on the ground a few feet from Valerie and her husband. He backhanded his hat from his head and began to work at his thick black hair with a pocket comb.

Not yet twenty, Billy had a sharp face, sharp features and soulless eyes, bluer than his father's and somehow much older. He wore an expensive white silk shirt with a string tie, a corduroy vest and whipcord trousers he'd had tailored for himself. His holster was handtooled, as were his high-heeled boots. He wore a gold chain across his vest and his belt buckle showed a carved longhorn head.

"That's right, ma'am. But don't you worry none. Men without women are plentiful out here."

Valerie heard him through the shock. She turned and stared at Billy, agony rolling in her green eyes.

"Please." She looked at them. "Can't you help him? Can't you do something for him?"

Hardhead Charley laughed coldly. "Looks like we'd be doing him a favor, not cutting that bullet out of him."

"What are you talklng about?"

"About them Apaches, ma'am. Seems to me your husband wasn't the bravest critter I ever laid eyes on the first time they attacked — and our horses were alive then. When they come back next time, looks like he'd be happy to be already dead."

14

She slapped the back of her hand against her mouth, chewed at it, staring at him.

Hardhead's voice was loud in the silent valley. "You don't think they're through with us, do you? They'll be back. But if they'd knowed what a looker you are, they'd be back even quicker."

She looked around helplessly, her face muscles rigid.

"We — can't just let him die," she whispered.

Hardhead Charley pumped an empty cartridge from his rifle chamber.

"Maybe you can't, ma'am," he said. "We ain't got time for fool things. We got to get ready for company. Because don't ever think we ain't going to have it."

Young Billy Clinton stopped combing his hair. He stood up, tall, lean and dandy. He set his hat crookedly on his head, staring toward the ridge to the north.

"Pa. Somebody's coming."

"Looks like an army wagon," Perch said, moving beside Billy. "Got red crosses on the side — see that from here."

"Army wagon." Hardhead Charley laughed. "That means the army is coming."

Young Billy shook his head. "I don't think so, Pa. That wagon is all by itself."

"Army wagon, out here alone? Don't be a jackass, boy."

"Might sound crazy to you, Pa. But that's what it is. One wagon, traveling slow. All by itself."

"And just one man," Perch said in weary disgust, "riding the boot. Don't look like this is the day for miracles, Hardhead."

# 2

BLADE MERRICK closed his fists, tightening the reins so the plodding army horses stopped near the burning wagon, shying slightly at the odor and the dead animals.

He had taken in the tragic picture all the way down the incline, with only the shoes of his horses as they cracked the alkali crust giving any sound to the whole world.

He saw the woman crouched in the sun with the man's head in her lap. From the distance, she was just a woman, and his gaze moved quickly from her to the three hardcases who had stepped around the charred remains of the wagon and stood waiting for him, squinting.

He gave a final scrape at his shirt front with his thumb.

"You folks making camp?" he inquired. His mouth was twisted into a bitter smile.

The teenager's eyes blazed, and he stiffened. Before he could speak, the older man caught his arm.

"A man stops where he has to." His voice was soft. "Where's the rest of the army?"

"Not more than two days' ride," Merrick said. "That way." He jerked his head in the direction he had come. He let his gaze move over the dead horses. "Might take you a mite longer afoot."

"Oh, well, we got plenty of time," Hardhead Charley said. But the tensions in his face belied his tone. "You hate people, ridin' alone out here this way?"

"I don't hate people," Merrick said. "But seems they just can't stand having *me* around."

"Where you heading?"

"South. Mission at San Carlos. You folks come from that way?"

"Yes," Perch Fisher said.

Anger showed under the surface of the older man's mild voice. "Well, we come from that direction. Like you can see, mister, we can stand jawing with you

18

in this here sun the rest of the day. But we'd take it most kindly if you'd help get us to hell out of here."

"Them Apaches ain't gone far," Billy Clinton said.

"Anyway, not far enough," Perch Fisher said. "So let's cut the jawing."

"Just a minute, boys," Hardhead Charley Clinton said. "We'd be mighty beholden to this gentleman for help. But this is kind of a tough spot. We want him to make up his own mind if'n he cares to pause here long enough to aid us."

The big man's polite tone may have deceived the other men, but Blade Merrick wasn't fooled. He realized that the bearded man knew they were doing their talking below the surface banter. They had scarcely pulled their gazes apart since they first had locked in that moment low-voiced greeting.

Merrick drew the back of his hand across his mouth. This man wasn't the polite type — not unless the hostiles had improved his disposition by scaring religion into him. Merrick doubted this.

The big man wanted help, wanted to get out of this inferno, but he was stepping cautiously, a barefoot man in a patch of sidewinders.

Merrick frowned faintly. The big man's face was the kind seen on reward posters. He'd seen him somewhere before, but couldn't place him for the moment.

He waited, licking his parched lips. He was being weighed, too. The big man had lived a long time. Indian attack was not his only worry — trouble awaited him in the civilized spots of this territory. He wanted to know how much Merrick knew about him before he made his next move. One thing sure, the big man would kill him in a second. He was already considering it.

He saw Clinton nod almost imperceptibly at the other big man. Perch walked with elaborate casualness around the horses, as if admiring horseflesh. This put Perch on one side of the wagon, the Clintons, father and son, on the other.

"Better just hold what you got," Merrick said to Perch. "Right there."

Perch looked wounded. "Why? What's the matter?"

Merrick shrugged. He moved deliberately, taking his Colt from its holster and laying it on the seat beside him, his hand covering it. He said, "I'd just like to say a couple things to you men." He stared at old Clinton.

"Why, feel free to say anything you like," Clinton said.

"It's about these army horses," Merrick said. "They'll pull far. But not fast. I figure three men could take turns doubling on one horse. They might get quite a ways — if they wasn't chased by Indians. Like I said, these horses couldn't outrun a little old lady, empty-saddled."

Clinton was silent a moment. His mouth pulled into a grimace. He was thinking, hard.

"The other thing is," Merrick said very softly, "if three men were to draw on me — all at once — wouldn't be but two of them left needing horses, and I'd figure to get the older one — the leader.

21

You see how that would be."

Clinton licked his whiskered mouth. "Whatever give you them inhospitable thoughts we might attack you?"

Merrick exhaled. "Maybe I wasn't thinking about you folks at all," he said, keeping his voice very low. "Maybe I was considering what I might be tempted to do if I was alone out on a wilderness with a woman and a wounded man — and some loner came along with a couple horses."

"Don't know what ever gave you that thought," Clinton said.

"Of course if this lady is your daughter," Merrick said. "I'm wrong right from the start."

"We never saw 'em before," Billy said.

"Shut up, Billy," Clinton said. He was looking at the heavy-shod army horses, at the wagon, and at the pink-plumed dust where the Indians rode.

Perch had moved again, so it was difficult for Merrick to see him at all and watch either of the men on the other side of the wagon.

22

He kept his voice friendly. "I'll have to ask you to stop right where you are. In fact," he stared hard at Clinton, "I think you better ask your friend to come back around there with you. I mean if you want to keep this whole thing friendly."

"Perch." Clinton spoke the word sharply. Perch laughed and walked slowly back to him, trailing the flat of his hand along the horse's flank as he walked.

Merrick sighed, shoving the gun back in its holster.

"See you got a casualty there for yourself," Merrick said, glancing at the man sprawled on the ground.

"It's nothing," Hardhead Charley Clinton told him. "Just a belly wound. Won't hurt him much if'n he don't laugh sudden."

"Or drink any hot coffee," Billy Clinton said. He tilted his hat slightly.

"Shut up, Billy." The older man's voice had iron in it.

Merrick pulled his gaze to the boy, and to the heavy-set jasper siding him. Nothing in their faces gave him anything to cheer about. The teenager had followed somebody too far along the owl-hoot trail. There was nothing in his mind now but self-indulgence, and a reputation he was going to build with the gun thonged at his thigh.

The cold stare of the other young man gave Merrick a slight chill at the nape of his neck. Here was a man who pulled wings off flies to watch them die, slowly.

"Like you can see," Old Clinton said, "the Indians have burned our wagon, killed all our horses."

"Probably plan to eat them when they come back," Merrick said.

"Please. Please help me."

The woman's voice had agony in it, and the fevered tenors of all she'd endured.

"Please help me."

Merrick said to Clinton. "Pardon me?"

"Shore," Clinton said. He and the other two stepped back enough so Merrick could spring to the ground beside them.

For a moment he faced them, hat

pushed back on his forehead. In dark trousers and sweated gray shirt, he appeared slender beside the two big men, but his leanness was corded muscle, and they saw this. They stepped back, watching him stride to the woman.

She looked up, and Merrick paused, catching his breath. Men always did this the first time they saw Valerie Butler, whether it was on a crowded dance floor, or out in the middle of the wastes.

Merrick breathed deeply. Once, a long time ago, he'd gone head-on into the butt of an army rifle. It was something like that now. He could have staggered under the impact of her. Not even the desert sun could spoil the soft smoothness of her skin or dull the fire of her hair.

He frowned. What was a woman like this doing with men like these hardcases?

She stared up at him. "My husband is dying."

He knelt beside her, pushing the looks of her and the smell of her out of his mind. He kept the wounded man's prostrate body between him and the three gunslingers, glancing up at them frequently. He pulled away the man's shirt and stared at the raw tear made by the bullet. He heard the woman's intake of breath.

"Got himself a nasty one," Merrick said. "Deep, too."

"Can you help him?"

"Might. If I could cut the bullet out."

"Please"

"That would take some time."

"Hell with that," Old Clinton said. "Let's get out of here before we all croak of lead poisoning."

The girl's eyes had filled with tears. She was staring into Merrick's face, silently pleading.

He kept his voice level. "Your friend has got a good point there, ma'am. If we can keep this fellow alive until we get to a safer spot, we'd all be a lot better off."

"Let's get out of here," Perch Fisher said.

Merrick stood up, facing the three

men across the girl and her prostrate husband.

"That's up to her," he said. "This here is her husband. It's up to her. She better know — it might kill him to move him."

"Going to kill us all not to move," Clinton said.

Perch Fisher's hand flexed, inches from his holster. "Ain't no question about it. We say we're moving out. That about settles it. She can get another husband — ain't many of us can grow a new scalp."

Merrick said, "Move your hand away from your gun, mister. And keep it away from it. If I hadn't come along, you people would've got scalp treatments anyhow.'

"But now you brought horses, mister," Perch said. "That changes things."

"They're my horses."

"Three of us got guns, though, say them horses belong to us."

"You move an inch nearer that gun, mister, we're going to have to cut lead

27

out of you," Merrick said. His temper
had blazed suddenly; his face grew hot
and his eyes were dry, fixed on Perch
Fisher and his poised gunhand.

Old Clinton spoke loudly. "Perch,
don't be a fool." After a moment, he
said, lowering his voice, "Now, Mrs.
Butler. It ain't reasonable to stay here
in this place and wait to be killed. If
we can get to some kind of shelter,
we can get that bullet out of your
husband."

The wounded man's lips parted. He
tried to speak. She knelt close. Then she
looked up, eyes stricken.

"Water. He wants some water."

Clinton stared at Merrick. "You got
any water?"

"I'm out. Water hole up the way is a
stop I planned to make."

"I got a canteen of water," Billy
Clinton said. "We can give him some
of that — if it ain't too far to the
water hole."

"It's not far," Merrick said. "Patchee
Wells. Few miles off the trail. Only water

I know during the dry spell."

Billy brought a canteen from the saddle of one of the dead horses. He knelt beside Valerie and tilted Butler's head while she held the canteen against his lips.

"Good you know this country," Clinton said. "We wouldn't last long without water. Drank up all ours during today's hot spell."

Merrick glanced at him over his shoulder. "You know Patchee Wells?"

"Can't say we do," Clinton said, voice loud.

Merrick knelt beside the wounded man again. "If he can hold on until we can get to the water hole, ma'am, we can fix him."

"All right," she said. Still dazed and unaware of what she was doing, she gave him young Clinton's canteen and stood up.

Merrick stood up, too. He extended the canteen toward the boy, then drew it back. "Mind if I have a drink?"

"You know how far it is to that

29

water hole, mister," the boy said. "Help yourself."

Merrick took one long drink of the water. He removed the canteen from his mouth, touched his tongue along his lips. He replaced the cap, handed it back to the boy. He frowned, staring at the canteen, but he did not say anything.

"We best get to goodbilly hell out of here," Hardhead Charley said, staring across the sun-baked flats.

Valerie Butler was staring at Merrick's canvas-covered wagon with the red crosses smeared hastily on its side. She shook her head, her voice still awed. "But you are alone," she said.

"That's right, ma'am."

She looked at him, puzzled. "Why were we attacked?" She looked at the three hardcases, at her husband, brought her gaze back to Merrick. "Yet you can travel alone across this Indian country and not be attacked?"

A shadow flickered across Merrick's face. He felt the gazes of the three men on him, saw the swirling lights the girl's eyes.

His mouth tightened. It was a long story. He didn't have time for it now.

He kept his tone light, his voice level as he let his glance touch the dead animals. "Maybe the Apaches figure army horses ain't fit to eat."

# 3

A HOT wind blew east across the valley, carrying a thin film of alkali dust stirred by the Indians. The sun had slid west of its apex, but none of its heat had lessened.

Merrick glanced at the woman, wondering when she would break. She was only holding herself together through some hidden will.

He frowned. It would be a lot better if she had a screaming, raging cry for herself. Merrick had seen what bottled agony could do to human beings.

He squinted west, searching for the Indians. The land lay flat and gray and silent, touched faintly with settling dust, glistening in the sun. The Apaches had disappeared. There was no sign of them. But he knew them too well. As far as he was concerned they were the smartest warriors the world had ever known. Just because you didn't see them didn't mean much.

He wasted no time. He vaulted into the rear of the wagon. It smelled like an overheated hospital ward under the canvas. At that, the woman's husband would he better off in here than broiling in that sun. He cleared away as many boxes as possible, stacking them against the support ribbing. He spread a blanket on the bed of the wagon, got down from the rear.

"All right," he said. "You men can move him into the wagon."

Billy Clinton moved to obey without question. He paused only long enough to toss one glance toward the distant dust.

After a slight hesitation, Old Clinton moved to the wounded man's boots.

Perch Fisher did not move. He stood watching Merrick with a twisted smile.

"Get your arms under his back, fellow," Merrick said "Don't get him bleeding any worse."

Clinton spoke sharply. "Perch. Get to

hell here and give us a hand."

Perch wasted just enough time to strike his gaze hard against Merrick's.

Merrick shrugged. *"It's your scalp, mister."*

He led the woman to the front of the wagon, helped her into the seat. He looked around, but all of her belongings had been consumed in the wagon fire.

The three men lifted Jeff Butler carefully into the wagon bed with Merrick watching them.

His voice was sardonic. "Makes you feel good to be able to do something for a man, don't it, men?"

Old Clinton laughed, but Perch stepped away from the wagon, eyes cold.

Clinton backhanded Perch across the bicep. "Come on, Perch. Get your saddle bag."

They moved hurriedly then, cutting their thick saddle bags free from their dead mounts. Carrying their rifles and the tightly-buckled saddle bags, they returned to the wagon.

Billy clambered up on the front seat

beside Valerie. Perch watched them, face expressionless.

"All right, mister," Old Clinton said. "Turn them horses around and let's get out of here."

Merrick had started toward the front of the wagon. He stopped, turned. He jerked his head south. "Water hole's that way — and that's the way were going."

Perch sprang forward. "Now you get this. I'm getting sick of you telling us' — "

He stopped in midair, facing Merrick's drawn gun. Merrick held it low, waiting.

Perch Fisher paled slightly.

Clinton laughed again, loudly. "All right, Perch. In the wagon. We can discuss our route later. Like the gentleman says, the important thing is gettin' to the water hole and gettin' the lead out of that poor wounded man."

Billy Clinton laughed. "The important thing is that gun in his hand, ain't it, Pa?"

Fisher shrugged his shirt up on his thick-slab shoulders. He backed away, never taking his gaze from Merrick's face.

Clinton waited until Perch had swung into the rear of the wagon. His voice was tea-party polite. "We're mighty beholden to you for all you're doing for us, mister . . . Uh, I don't believe, I caught your name."

"Blade Merrick."

There was an odd tightening about Clinton's mouth so that his scraggly beard wiggled slightly.

"You heard of me?" Merrick asked.

Clinton had not stopped smiling. "No, sir. Not that I recall."

He hoisted himself into the rear of the wagon beside Perch Fisher.

Merrick glanced once more toward the boulders west of them and then swung up beside Valerie Butler.

She sat rigidly, her gaze fixed on something deep inside her own mind. Merrick glanced across her at Billy Clinton. Billy shook his head. She was pretty far gone.

36

Merrick took up the reins, slapped them across the rumps of the horses.

The animals strained forward. They were only slightly faster than army mules would have been, though Major Brackett had given him horses to help speed him south.

"Can't these critters move any faster?" Billy Clinton said.

"Not built for speed," Merrick said. Valerie Butler had sagged slightly. He felt the pressure of her shoulder against his arm. Even though he realized she was unaware of what she was doing, he felt the warmth of her against him.

His mouth pulled into its bitter semblance of a smile. *It has been a long time. Never one so lovely as this.*

Billy was watching the west end of the valley, but he did not mention the Indians. He didn't have to. They were in both their minds.

"Blade Merrick," the boy said. "My name's Billy Clinton. The bearded old goat is my pa. Hardhead Charley Clinton. Maybe you've heard of him?"

Merrick nodded without turning his gaze from the way south. He'd been right again — Hardhead Charley's face was on reward posters back at Fort Ambush.

The silence, broken only by the crackling earth crunching under the horses' hooves, deepened. Billy said, "You an army man, Merrick? I mean, you got the wagon, and I seen army supplies. But no uniform."

"Working for them right now. Sometimes I scout. But mostly, I work for myself. I'm a hunter."

"That so? What do you hunt?"

Merrick did not answer. Billy Clinton caught his breath just faintly, shrugged his shirt up on his shoulders.

Valerie Butler swayed slightly between them.

"Watch her," Merrick told Billy. "She might faint."

"I'm all right," the woman said. "How far is it to this water hole?"

"Not far, ma'am. Just hope the Indians didn't circle around this way."

"I don't think so," Billy answered him.

"I been watching. I seen no sign."

Merrick's laugh was short. "You pretty good at reading Indian signs, boy?"

"I'm good enough. Pa and Perch and me have moved around right under their noses when we had to. We used the same water holes. And it was me that knew where they were, and what they was doing."

"Takes a smart man."

"I'm smart enough."

"I wasn't ribbing you, boy. I meant it. I admire a man can live in Indian country and keep his scalp."

Billy laughed, pleased at the praise. "Wasn't real good living. No gunfire, no fires. You don't have things real comfortable."

They plodded forward some moments in silence. Merrick told himself to forget the smell of the woman, the warmth of her touching him. She was ill with shock. If she fell into his arms, it would mean nothing. Just the same his heart slugged faster at the warm scent of her hair.

He spoke to Billy. "You know this country, eh?"

Billy opened his mouth to speak, closed it. After a moment, he said, "We were just passing through."

"But you get this way — often?"

"Any man who'd travel this country when he didn't have to is crazy."

Merrick stared across the girl's red hair at the boy. "But sometimes a man has to, eh?"

Billy's gaze met his levelly. As plainly as words, the boy's eyes told him he was pushing it, that he might as well save his breath.

Billy shrugged.

After a moment, Billy said, "You been in Tucson lately? Lordsburg?"

"Few weeks ago."

"Man. I miss them spots. We been down on the border, but it ain't the same. They tell you a woman is a woman. But I like Tucson. I like noise. I like excitement. What's new up that way?"

40

"Depends on how long you been away," Merrick said. A small muscle worked in the hard line of his jaw. "'Bout a month ago, bank was robbed at Tucson."

Billy laughed, staring at him. He shrugged his shirt up on his shoulders again. He said, "I don't mean that kind of news. I mean, any new women up there, anything like that."

"I don't know. You'll have to wait until you get up there and see."

"Man. I will." He let his gaze graze unhurriedly over Valerie Butler. "Mrs. Butler here is the first white woman I've seen in — a long time. Too long. A man can get mighty thirsty, you know, Merrick?"

The jolt of the wagon thrust her hard against him again. Merrick's hand tightened on the reins. He slapped them across the horses. "Yeah," he said.

Billy Clinton laughed. "Her husband. He's a real dude. They got lost, he told us, couple days ago. Here they were, alone in that wagon, and Apaches trailing them.

That's when we caught up with them this morning."

The woman made a sound deep in her throat. Both of them stared at her, but her gaze was fixed on nothingness. She seemed unaware of them.

Billy said, "I'd been seeing Indian sign for hours. They ain't too smart — if you're smart. My old woman was part Mescalero. Them Apaches were after anything that moved. Like you said, they're eatin' horses this summer. They were after us, too. It was a question there. We didn't know what to do. Traveling with the wagon would slow us down — "

"They could catch you anyway — if they decided to."

Billy nodded, shrugged. "We considered that. And the Butlers' wagon offered the only shield in case they did attack. They had it loaded. Mrs. Butler said it was everything she owned — man, that husband of hers hadn't bought her much. So — anyhow we threw in with them. It was just as well. We stumbled into an

Apache ambush just before noon. We outran them into the valley — and that was a mistake. We got out there in the open, and the first thing they did was to shoot our horses and burn the wagon."

Merrick nodded. "Makes sense. They could always come back for you people."

# 4

**M**ERRICK slowed the horses to
a walk and then halted them on
the rise above Patchee Wells.

"How about it?" he said to Billy. "You
smell Apache?"

"Think we better scout before we ride
in?"

"If they're here, they knew we were
coming. They've had time to bake us a
cake."

Billy Clinton stood up on the wagon.
He gave his hat a rakish tilt, caught
his thumbs in his belt, moving his
head slowly.

The water holes called Patchee Wells
were in a depression, with the bubbling
water against a wall making a short fall
to a second level and then a drop into the
sump. From the lowest part of the ground
the earth rose upward forming a broken

cup with the water at its bottom. Above the rim were twisted piñon, gnarled joshua trees, a beard of mesquite that petered out into the barren hills and flatland so a man could pass within a mile of the water hole and die of thirst without even knowing it was there.

A soothing balm of cool rose from the sump and the silence deepened inside it. The largest pool was clear and deep with rock formations misshapen through the water.

"Lets go in," Billy said.

Merrick nodded, slapped the reins. The horses cleared the rise and then he drove the wagon downslope to within a few feet of the lower pool.

Clinton and Perch Fisher leaped from the wagon. Fisher flopped to the water's edge, buried his face in it, came blowing.

"Let's get this man out of the wagon," Merrick said, swinging down.

He saw Billy helping the woman from the seat, watched the boy's hands travel swiftly, hungrily over her body.

He climbed into the wagon bed, lifted

45

Butler's shoulders. Billy and Old Clinton took the wounded man's legs. Carefully, taking their time, they lifted him out to the ground.

Merrick spread a blanket and they placed Butler on it. Merrick tore away his shirt.

Valerie knelt at the head of the blanket, staring at her youthful husband's bloodless face.

Merrick felt a sharp twist in his solar plexus. This Jeff Butler was a handsome devil, with straight, even features and curly hair. No doubt he was a devil with the women. Plainly enough, his wife was enslaved.

Merrick's voice was sharper than he'd intended. "Billy, loose those horses, water them and stake them in that grass patch."

"Sure, mister," Billy said. Merrick didn't look around.

Hardhead Charley said, "It's an uphill climb for them horses, in case we have to get out of here in a hurry."

"Don't get yourself in a bind, Clinton,"

46

Merrick said. "That wagon could be seen from miles on the ridge. Put it in the mesquite and it's too far away from us. Them Apaches come back, likely we won't have time to get in the wagon."

Valerie said, "Is he alive?"

Merrick tested Butler's pulse, found it weak. "He's hanging on," he told her. He glanced up at Clinton. "There's antiseptic in that wagon, some gauze and bandages. Would you get it?"

Clinton moved to the wagon, pawed around inside it.

"You, Fisher, build a fire," Merrick said. He removed his knife, tested it against his cheek. Finding a smooth boulder, he began working the blade against it.

"You build the goddam fire yourself," Fisher said "Clintons can take orders from you if they want to."

With the knife in his hand, Merrick came up to his feet. His heart was slugging, the blood congealed in the pit of his stomach. He felt the rage from the backs of his knees upward.

It would take very little to make him attack any one of these three. Nobody had to tell him Old Clinton and Fisher had plotted his death all the way across the badlands.

Clinton swung around from the wagon. His voice struck the sump walls, rebounded. "Damn you to goodbilly hell, Perch. I warned you. You simmer your pot, fast, boy. You build that fire like he says."

For an instant, everything in the silent world of the water hole seemed holding its breath. Perch Fisher kept his hand clawed out over his gun. His sunscorched face was paled, and a pulse worked in his throat.

Merrick stood there gripping the knife. He had seen Fisher's kind in every saloon west of El Paso. A man on the prod, carrying a chip on his shoulder, feeling degraded the moment some man didn't share his own high estimate of himself. He could take a beating easier than he could take orders. And there was more. He was a man who notched his guns, thonged them down, and got almost a sexual excitement from using them. But he was a big man, too, and he got another thrill from inflicting physical pain. He would beat a man's face in in a fist fight, and few cowmen cared for that kind of combat. But then, Merrick knew he had not for a moment considered Perch Fisher a cowman.

Fisher looked Merrick over, laughed. "Sure, friend."

"You can gather some greasewood sticks," Merrick said, aware his voice reflected his own inner rage, though he kept it low. "Makes a faster fire."

He knelt beside Butler again, whetting his knife on the stone.

Butler was rolling his head slowly back and forth. His eyes were closed, and though he was burning with fever, his flesh was dry and his clothes were not sweated. He was talking swiftly, but his words were unintelligible.

Her head bent, Valerie was watching

her husband. She tried to smooth his hair back from his forehead, but he twisted away from her, speaking in that fevered monotone.

Fisher tossed some greasewood sticks to the ground near them, and slapped his shirt, seeking matches.

"Don't build that fire in the open," Merrick said.

"Why not?"

"How have you stayed alive this long?"

Fisher laughed. "By being just a little better than the next man I meet, Merrick."

"You got to be smarter than the Apaches to get out of this one."

"You think they don't know we're at this water hole?"

Merrick kept his voice low. "There's still a chance they don't know. They know they left you at that wagon, without horses. They might not know you got this far."

"Them horses of yours left shoe tracks."

"They'll find them — when they get back to your dead horses. Meantime, no sense telling them we're here. This water hole is known to mighty few white men."

Clinton stood there with the medical supplies and bandages.

"Right," he said. "That might give us a little time. If they think we don't know about this place."

Merrick jerked his head toward the overhanging boulder and the sheltered place beneath it. "Build a small fire over there."

Fisher and Billy Clinton built a fire. By that time Merrick had spread out the medicines and supplies he would need on the blanket beside Butler.

He got up then, crossed to the fire. Perch was whispering to Billy as he approached. Perch stopped talking and looked up, grinning.

Merrick stared at the thick-jowled man. *Fine. I have less to fear from the Apaches than from these hardcases.*

He jabbed the knife into the hottest part of the fire, and held it there.

They watched him walk back to the blanket.

Valerie cradled her husband's head against her breasts.

"You better not watch," Merrick said.

She stared up at him. "I'm all right."

Old Clinton pressed his weight against Butler's shoulders and upper arms. Sweat popped out across the old pirate's forehead as he watched Merrick's knife probe deeper and deeper through the layers of Butler's flesh.

Blood spurted suddenly, erupting from the man's side. He heard Valerie gasp, saw her tighten her hands about her husband's head.

Butler stiffened, and then sagged, unconscious.

"That's fine," Clinton said.

Using gauze wrapped around his fingers, Merrick worked the bullet out against the knife blade.

He dropped the knife, the pellet of lead and the strings of blood on the blanket.

Valerie was rocking back and forth, pressing Butler's head against her breasts, crooning something unintelligible.

Merrick glanced up at Clinton. "Too bad she won't join him."

"I could clip her on the jaw," Clinton stated, matter-of-factly. "I got nothing against hittin' a woman."

Merrick was pouring the antiseptic over the wound, reaching for the dressing. He glanced up briefly, his mouth twisted. "In her condition, you'd be taking a chance. If you didn't knock her out first time, she might beat hell out of you."

Clinton laughed, twisting Butler's inert body so that Merrick could bandage it. "Wouldn't be the first time some woman belted me. I've had me a mite of trouble with women in my time. Never met one yet that would fight fair."

With Butler bandaged and laid out in the shade of the wagon, there was nothing to do but wait for him to regain consciousness or die from shock.

Clinton replaced the medical supplies in the wagon and went to the overhang. He kicked out the fire, trampling the ashes under his boot.

Merrick cleaned the knife blade by thrusting it into the sand several times. He picked up the small lead pellet, studying it. It was blunted and shapeless. He dropped it on the blanket beside Butler. He might like a souvenir.

He walked down to the pool, washed up.

Hunkered beside the clear pool, he stared at himself for a moment, seeing the reflected piñon, the boulders, and the sky. He moved his gaze to the three men under the overhang. Hardhead Charley was propped against the stone wall with Perch lounging on his left and young Billy flat on his back to Clinton's right.

He stared at them for a long time, his mouth taut. Then he looked at Valerie Butler and her husband. Butler was still unconscious. Valerie was leaning against a wagon wheel, motionless.

He sighed, washing the blood from between his fingers, immersing his hands and then shaking them dry.

54

Clinton said, "Merrick."

Merrick walked up the slight incline and stood under the rock overhang. The three men stared up at him, old Clinton openly, Perch through hooded eyes, and Billy with a faint grin from beneath his hat.

"You done a fine job, Merrick." Clinton nodded toward Butler. "That shore ain't the first bullet you ever dug out of a man."

"No."

"We figure now the bullet is out, it's time to hightail it out of here."

"Apaches," Billy said, grinning. "Remember?"

Merrick waited.

Clinton said, "Way I figure it, once them Apaches come back to eat our horses, won't take them a coon's age to trail us here."

Merrick scraped his thumb joint against his shirtfront.

"So, if we want to get to Fort Ambush with our scalps, we best hit the road," Clinton said.

Merrick let his gaze move from one to the other, and finally back to Hardhead Charley.

"I thought I told you men. I'm not headed to Fort Ambush. I came from there."

"Just where do you plan to go?" Clinton kept his voice level.

"I'm on my way to the mission at San Carlos. There's a fever epidemic. They need these medicines. That's where I'm going. You men want to go with me, you're welcome."

Clinton glanced at Billy and then at Perch. Suddenly Perch burst out laughing. Billy pulled the hat over his face and Clinton stared up at Merrick, grinning.

# 5

OLD CHARLEY drew in a deep breath, staring at Merrick. But before he could speak Billy sat up, his hat toppling forward. Billy touched Old Charley's arm and shook his head at him, warningly.

"What's the matter, boy?" Hardhead said.

Billy whispered, "Apaches, Pa. I smell 'em."

Merrick saw the tensions swirl in the older man's eyes. Obviously, Hardhead Charley and Perch Fisher stayed alive in the Indian country by trusting young Billy's keen senses.

Merrick moved from the overhang, forgetting the veiled threat of the Clintons in the more urgent matter of the Apaches having found them already. He'd hoped for more time. He'd thought he had the situation pretty well figured: the Apaches had pulled away from the attack back there the valley to let the surviving white people stew in sun and fear while they prepared themselves through soul-cleansing ceremonies for a feast of roast horse, and for the warrior's pleasure of torturing white prisoners and enjoying the white man's woman before they killed her, or she died. Of course, he had been certain they would return after those ceremonies to the scene of the attack: their victims wouldn't get far on foot in that waste. He had believed that when they returned to the valley and found their victims had eluded them, they would pause to eat the horses. He was hoping he and the others had that many hours before the Apaches trailed them here to the Wells. There was no reason to hope they had that much time any more . . . not if Billy Clinton's instincts spoke truly.

Billy came forward to his knees, tapped his hat rakishly and got silently to his feet. Merrick watched, amazed at the Indian-stealth of the boy. There was not a creak of boot leather, rattle of spur or bump of gun against leather.

Billy glanced over his shoulder at his father and Perch Fisher.

"Stay right there. Don't breathe," he said. He turned his mocking gaze on Blade. "All right, Merrick. You know how to handle Indians, let's go handle them."

Billy crept up the incline and Merrick matched his cautious steps. They moved silently; any sounds in the dry breathless afternoon came from the camp behind them, the water below in the sump.

They crouched behind the boulders at the rim of the knoll above the water hole. For a long time they watched the piñon and mesquite tangled woods before them. Not even a breeze stirred in the underbrush. If there were men out there, they breathed as shallowly as Billy and Merrick.

They might have missed the Apache hidden in the underbrush, but his pony switched its tail at a fly. In that immense expanse of stillness this slight movement grabbed their gazes.

"There," Billy whispered. "Right in that underbrush."

"Probably got a rifle trained on us right now."

"One of us could stay here, other try to go around him."

"What makes you think he's alone?"

"What do you think?"

"As you do. He's likely a scout, sent up here to find out we're here. That case he's alone. Or it might be three or four."

"Either way I get impatient just sitting here waiting."

"Wait a minute. We got two chances. One is that even if he's got a rifle, he won't be as expert with it as with arrows or knives. If we can draw his fire, maybe we can disarm him."

"Disarm him?" Billy stared at him as if he were insane. "We'll kill him."

"Won't buy us much. I'd rather risk letting him have one shot."

"You said we had two chances." There was lack of enthusiasm in Billy's voice. "What's the other one?"

"The other one is that maybe he is a scout and is alone. If he's alone, he's scouting for the raiders. Maybe he don't want to fight. If he's a scout, his job is to find out about us and get back to report. If we let him get away — nobody has to get killed."

"You an Injun lover, Merrick?"

"No. I don't mind staying alive, though."

"I'm not about to let him go back and tell them where we are."

"Now you're loco. It's only a matter of time until they find us anyhow — without him. Our only hope is that we can get Butler out of here before then."

"That's your idea, mister. I say if it's a scout, let's try to outfox — and kill him — then get out of here, whether Butler enjoys the trip or not."

Merrick glanced at Billy. There was lust in young Clinton's eyes, more urgent now than when he had looked at Butler's wife. He had the lust to kill; you saw in that moment in his face what he had become, what he would be if he lived

61

fifty years or if this Indian killed him. He was a gun killer. He wanted another notch on his gun butt; an Indian made as good-looking a notch as a white man.

Merrick's mouth tightened. No sense in attempting to argue with Hardhead Charley's only whelp. If he could get Billy to moving away from him, hiding and running in an entrapment try that wouldn't deceive an Apache eight-year-old, it would give Merrick his only chance to work out something; a dead Indian would be dangerous to wear around their necks right now.

"Okay,"he said. "I'll go around this boulder far enough so the Indian can see me. You move out to the right there — keep moving way around. If he comes out enough to get a shot at me, maybe you can get him."

Billy nodded. Then his mouth twisted. "You trusting me pretty far, Merrick. You must know how bad we want you dead if you won't head north."

"Hell," Merrick said with a casualness he did not feel. "You don't want an

Indian to kill me, Billy. That wouldn't put any notches in your gun."

Billy looked him over, grudging admiration in his gaze.

"Okay," Billy said. He slithered to another boulder. "Take care of yourself."

Merrick moved around the boulder. He glanced at Billy, hoping he got a moment for palaver with the Indian. If he did maybe he could keep Billy from shooting. He didn't count on it.

Merrick gave a low call. Behind him he heard Billy stop, tensed. He was watching the underbrush, did not turn his head. He saw the brush rattle some yards away in a line between himself and the pony. There was a rocky clearing between the rim of the boulder and the edge of the mesquite beard.

Merrick said, "Friend." He repeated the word in the Mescalero dialect.

He showed himself, tense, ready to dive back to the concealment of the boulder.

He waited, holding his breath. The brush parted and the Apache warrior

63

stood up, face streaked with white and yellow paint-patterns, a rifle in his left hand.

Merrick stepped away from the boulder, showing himself. There was another breathless wait, the kind that rips a man's nerves to shreds, and then the Apache stepped forward.

Merrick squinted, staring at the Apache. There was something familiar about the warrior's face, but the hell of it was, he could not recall the Apache's name.

The Apache looked him over, standing tense, ready to spring back into the brush.

Merrick saw the look of recognition light the Apache's eyes. His faint smile was a fantastic thing in the painted face. Thank God, Merrick thought, this one knows me. This is the answer, the way out.

The Apache lifted his right hand in a gesture of friendliness, palm outward. His widening smile pulled at the yellow lines in his cheeks. He stepped forward, and at that moment Billy Clinton's forty-four cracked from behind the boulder to Merrick's right.

The Indian never even got a chance to stop smiling. Billy Clinton was a dead shot as well as a fast draw. The bullet struck the Apache in the chest and spun him around. The rifle toppled from his grasp. The Indian struck the ground on his knee, then turned to move away, trying to sprint toward his startled pony. He was already as good as dead, but Billy shot him again.

"Good work, Merrick," Billy shouted. "God knows you really pulled him right out in the open."

Merrick stared at Billy, eyes cold. Not even hidden from God in the night could Billy ever say he had not seen the rifle in the Indian's left hand, his upraised palm. He turned on his heel and ran across the rocky ground to the place where the Indian had fallen.

He knelt on one knee, turned the Indian over. All the rest of his life he would wish he had not done it. A moment more and the Indian would have been dead, and he would not have had to see the look of hatred and contempt on his painted face. Maybe the Apache didn't know the name Judas, but that was what the look in his black eyes named Merrick.

Perch Fisher and Hardhead Charley climbed the incline, ran out to where the Indian had been shot. He was dead by the time they got there.

Billy stood looking down at the Apache, still holding his forty-four.

"I killed him, Pa," Billy said.

Merrick stared up at Billy. "What you've done, boy, is just bought us a part of hell none of us will get out of."

Then, forgetting the Clintons, Merrick jerked his head around. He and Billy spoke simultaneously. "The pony."

"Grab that pony," Merrick said, staring toward the underbrush where they'd sighted it.

He jumped to his feet. Billy ran forward beside him, and then both stopped.

Standing side by side they watched

the pony race north in the flatland, pounding dust balls from the earth, trailing its single-strand hair-bridle.

Merrick pulled his gaze around. But it didn't seem to matter which way he turned, all he saw was trouble. The dead Indian lay contorted in the sun. Whatever chance they'd had to get out of here alive had died with him. Whatever tortures the Apaches had had in mind this morning would be intensified twenty times when they found the murdered scout.

"We got to get out of here," Billy Clinton said.

Merrick's laugh was cold. "You begin to see what you've done, boy?"

"Hell. You pulled him out so I could kill him, and I killed him."

"He had his hand raised, friendly. You recognized it."

"Maybe I know enough Indians I don't trust them."

Merrick shrugged. "Or maybe you got just enough white blood in you to make you mistrust everybody. But

67

it ain't buying us anything to worry about that now. When those Indians find that pony, they might even delay that feast of roast horse to come avenge this buck." He glanced at the insignia on the Indian's wristlet. "A well-born warrior — and that won't help, either."

"All right," Perch said. "You got sense enough to know that, let's go."

"Running won't help you or me, now. If we run, we'll kill Butler, and we still won't escape them. What we had was one chance in a thousand, and Billy-boy just shot that to hell." He paced back and forth, his boots harsh against the outcroppings of rock. "Billy, there are army spades in the back of that wagon. Bring 'em. Maybe we still got one chance — if we can bury your mistake."

When Billy brought the sharp-bladed spades, Merrick led them into the wooded area. He chose a mesquite bush and began digging about three feet out from its base. After a moment Old Clinton and Billy, seeing that he intended removing the bush in a solid clump of roots and earth, fell to digging.

They dug deeply under the roots. They didn't pause to breathe. Loosening a large clod of earth they carefully put their backs to it, lifted it from the hole and set it aside. The four of them dug then, excavating a five-foot rectangle, piling each spadeful of earth in neat piles at the rim of the open grave.

They lifted the Indian, lowered him into the earth, buried him with his rifle.

"Them Apaches won't like a white man burial for this buck any better than they'll like us killing their scout," Clinton said. That was his prayer and epitaph uttered over the open grave.

"I'm hoping we get out of here before they find him." Merrick mopped sweat from his face. They replaced the earth in the hole, stamping it down so that all the brown-colored underearth could be replaced. Finally, they lifted the mesquite bush, set it in place and repaired the scarred earth surface around it.

Merrick carefully scraped up all the telltale underearth remaining. He walked twenty paces into the forest, scattering it in the underbrush.

He returned, and with mesquite limbs they swept around the bush until there was no sign of their digging, no trace of their bootmarks. They walked on the balls of their feet back to the rock outcropping, dragging the brush after them.

They toppled to the shade of the overhang. Billy lay face down, panting. They stared at the water hole, at the sky, at each other. For a long time none of them spoke.

Billy sat up, flicking the chamber of his gun, reloading. "What now?"

"You tell me," Merrick said.

"Let's get out of here." Perch Fisher gathered up his gear and the tightly-stuffed saddle bags.

"Not a chance," Merrick said. "All we can do now is wait until either Butler gets well enough to travel, or the Apache finds us. If they don't learn we've killed the scout, we got one chance of leaving here alive."

"Hell." Perch laughed. "You wait, mister. But you wait by yourself." His voice rose, his taunting laughter striking at Merrick.

# 6

HARDHEAD CHARLEY picked up a burnt stick and traced lines along the ground beside him. Suddenly Perch Fisher stopped laughing, the sound ending abruptly. His face was chilled as though he'd never laughed, would never laugh again. It grew quiet under the overhang.

"I think you're wrong," Hardhead Charley said at last. "I don't like to dispute a smart young fellow like you, Mister Merrick, but there don't seem to me but one thing to do and that is to head north out of here and run like our tails was afire."

Perch got up on his haunches. His voice was blunt. "I can give it to you straighter than that, Merrick. A lot straighter. Now, we three don't intend going back to San Carlos. It's up to you after that. If you don't want to walk, you better change your mind."

Merrick stared at the pulse working in the stout man's throat. He sighed. The way the rages built in him at the sound of these men's voices was bad. It was as though he'd come to them with a built-in hate. It was hell when you stood there almost wishing that a man would go for his gun, or make a play.

He tightened his fists. He had to shake thoughts like these. He knew what made him hate these men all right, but intuition and instinct was not enough — if they were the men he sought, he'd been looking for them for a long time, and he had to have proof.

"Perch, do yourself a favor." He kept his voice low, hoping the inner rages didn't show. "Don't threaten me."

Perch came upward, standing with his back against the wall of the overhang. "There ain't no sense you and me delayin' any more, mister. You turn it to clabber with me — so if you don't like what I say, I'm more than anxious for you to make anything you want to out of it."

Merrick kept his voice low. "No use to kill each other yet, Perch. Butler is still too ill to travel. So unless he dies in the next couple hours, nobody's going anywhere."

Perch put his hand out at his side.

"You don't get the message. I'm not staying in this place until them Apaches scalp me."

The pulse throbbed in Fisher's neck. His gaze darted against the walls of the sump, to the wagon, and to the boulders and the rim of stunted trees beyond. Clearly, this depression was a trap as far as Perch Fisher was concerned, and they were in the deepest cranny of it.

"You got that clear, Merrick?" Fisher's voice shook. "We're clearing out."

Merrick's face changed too, in that moment. The cold hatred that contorted it when he looked at Perch Fisher became something hot and livid when he stared at this water hole. Perch scowled at what he saw in Merrick's face. Young Billy sat up and tilted his hat back on his head. Hardhead

Charley's eyes narrowed. The look is Merrick's face named this spot a hell, and his searing hatred included every grain of sand around it.

His voice quavered slightly when he spoke. "I got no wish to stay in this place one minute longer than I have to."

He exhaled, watching them. For a moment there was deep silence. They read it in his face — a man hates a place so it is agony to return to it: a place associated with deep hurt, or fear, or horror — maybe compounded of all of it. And they saw this in Blade Merrick's face. Until this moment they may not have considered him capable of fear. Now they knew better. Fear and hatred and horror, that was what this water hole meant to Blade Merrick.

Merrick turned and walked away from them. He stepped out of the shadowed overhang, squinting suddenly at the brassy brilliance of the sunlight.

Perch stepped away from the wall and his hand moved to his gun.

Merrick spun on his heel, crouching

and stepping to the left. It all happened so abruptly they were hardly aware his gun was in one hand and his other was spread above its hammer, ready to fan a spray of six rounds under that overhang.

Young Billy Clinton gasped. He had seen Merrick draw fast earlier, but it was nothing like this. Billy had watched trick-gun artists work for drinks along the border, but their speed was not this kind of speed.

Old Clinton's laugh was falsely hearty. "Why, man. Man," he said, "you got to trust us better than this, Mister Merrick. Why, which one of us would draw on you when your back was turned?"

Billy Clinton laughed. "After what I just seen, Pa, that's the only way I'm ever going to draw on him." He pushed off his hat and worked at his hair with a comb, grinning at his father and Perch Fisher.

Perch Fisher's face was white, and it was an effort for him to move his hand away from the butt of his gun. He let it slide back. He had not cleared leather, and for a moment he was almost paralyzed, realizing how close he'd come to dying. He managed to move his hand away and to breathe out slowly.

Merrick's face, too, was pale. His voice was cold. He ignored old Clinton, staring at Perch. "You breathe too loud, Fisher. You telegraph it. You give yourself away — you give yourself away, even when you mean to shoot a man in the back. Sometime, that's going to cost you your life."

Perch tried to laugh. His voice was loud. "If you're going to shoot, why didn't you shoot?"

Billy laughed. "I can tell you, Perch, if you're to stupid to know. He don't want to kill you — unless he has to. Not with a gun. Them Apaches ain't deaf."

"Go to hell, you little bastard."

Billy laughed again. "Pa, you gonna let him talk about your only son like that? Go on, Pa. Tell him. Tell him how you was married to Ma — by a full-blooded chief — with a gun in your back. Tell him."

"Shut up, Billy." Clinton walked out of the shadow. "Put away your gun, Mister Merrick. Perch meant nothing. We're all upset here. But Perch ain't going to shoot you. Not unless he gets the order from me . . . and I ain't going to give it."

Merrick shoved his gun back into its holster. He was trembling, and to hide it, he closed his fists. He stared at Hardhead Charley, let his gaze move to Billy and to Perch.

He turned on his heel and walked away then, going down the incline. Valerie Butler looked up, eyes dull, watching him stride past. His shadow lunged along the ground, and as he passed, she watched his shadow. He glanced at Jeff Butler only long enough to see he was breathing shallowly and that his eyes were closed. The bleeding had stopped; his outer bandage was not stained.

They watched him reach the ridge, and then he walked to the left and was out of sight.

He moved slower now, going down the incline.

He stayed alert, listening. He had seen in the faces of the Clintons and Perch what they meant to do. Within minutes after arriving at the place where the Indian attack had left them horseless, he'd known Clinton was weighing the chances of killing him, taking the army horses and abandoning the Butlers to the Apaches. He had stopped them there. But there had been more than that: Clinton had known the Indians would come back. The army dray horses were slow and plodding; the three of them couldn't hope to escape the attackers on two mounts, in the desert, without water. It had seemed better sense to keep Merrick alive, another gun against the raiders. They had let him live because they had been sure they could kill him when they found it convenient.

He gave a short hard laugh. Wasn't that moment going to come the first time he closed his eyes to sleep?

His fists clenched at his sides. Well,

he wasn't going to sleep, because they were not the only men out here looking for something.

He paused beside a mound of earth. The earth turned up here was so fresh the plants hadn't covered it yet, a few blades of grass, the prickled head of a sweet cactus. He knew how fresh this mound was — he'd turned it up making a grave deep enough to foil the digging coyotes. The only marker he'd left was a small cross formed with stones. They were untouched.

This grave was one month old.

Merrick knelt beside the mound, fists knotted at his sides. His mouth was a taut line.

He braced himself suddenly at the sharp sound of Billy's laughter down in the sump.

# 7

A MONTH ago he had ridden expectantly into this hidden water hole.

"Ab!" He had called even before he swung out of the saddle. Only a month, but it seemed longer. He felt so much older now, full of urgent hatred where before there had been only the day's troubles and the hurt of a loss, that, great as it was, was old and at least covered with scar tissue. He felt old now. Older than the devil himself.

"Ab!"

He was still calling his brother when he dismounted and ground-tied his mount in the grass clump. He had even laughed a little. Ab trusted nobody any more. Still, it didn't make sense that be would hide around here until he was certain Blade was alone.

He almost stumbled on Ab's body.

He stared down at the body and first there was nothing but disbelief. It couldn't be Ab, and Ab couldn't be dead. But it was Ab, and his death was brutal and senseless. Somebody had emptied a six-shooter into him, willfully and crazily, firing after Ab was already dead because whoever he was, he got a sensual pleasure from slamming bullets into a human body.

After the first wild grief passed, a chill went through Blade Merrick's body. He walked slowly about the water hole, going over it carefully, with deadly purpose.

The day was dry and breathless. The sun glittered in the clear pool and something skittered through the mesquite. Ab was sprawled near the largest pool, and the blood had made a round dark place in the sand where it ran from his mouth. He had been kicked repeatedly.

Blade had stood there, trembling. Had they kicked him before he died or after? Knowing Ab, he was sure it must have been after they'd put bullets into him.

Somebody had gotten a lot of pleasure from this killing.

Blade stood rigid. They'd pulled off Ab's boots, ripped his shirt away, left his body to the sun and the ants.

That was when Blade made the next discovery. Though they'd ripped away his clothes and kicked him, filled him with lead, it was all a senseless killing. They had not robbed him. They hadn't even taken the change from his pockets.

Why had they killed Ab?

To this day Blade Merrick did not know.

He had stood there in the clearing beside Ab's body trying to find the answer to the meaningless killing. He had stared at the coppery sky, demanding to know. He had searched the rocks, the water, the wooded places. There was no answer.

It had been a reasonless, senseless killing. In this long month Merrick had tried to think out some reason for it. Only one occurred to him: these three men had come unexpectedly upon Ab; they had been spoiling with the need and pleasure of killing, and they had told themselves they did not want to leave a witness to their trail south from Patchee Wells.

He had strode about the place, a man mad with his anger. If there had been a reason for killing, they would have robbed him. They would have taken time to search him.

It was sure they didn't know Ab. There was nothing personal in the killing. It was something done hurriedly and without profit. They had killed Ab as they would kill a tarantula on a hot rock, and then had ridden hurriedly on after they'd watered their horses and filled their canteens.

Blade had removed his brother's belongings from his pockets and piled them on a handkerchief: a wallet, a Mexican gold piece, some silver money, and Blade's letter that had tortuously searched him out on the border.

Hunkered beside the body, Blade read the letter he'd written to Ab. It had taken a long time for that letter to find Ab.

It had been a much longer time before Blade received his reply.

Dear Ab:

I'm writing you this letter because I've good news. At least it is good to me, and it will be to you if you'll pocket your crazy stubborn Virginia pride and admit the war between the Confederacy and the Union is over — and has been over for years.

I better tell you, Ab, that despite the fact the war is over, the United States considers you a pretty formidable enemy. They've a list of crimes charged against you longer than my arm, starting with your escape from the Yankee prison in Ohio. It's hard for them to forgive the robberies charged to you along the border because a lot of them have been against the government.

But I've a good record with them, Ab. After the war, I came back out here and worked with the Indian agency, and with the army. I've made some good friends, and I've used every one of them trying to square things so you can go back home a free man.

Anyhow there's a full pardon awaiting you at Tucson.

You have only to report, take an oath of loyalty to the United States, and it's yours.

Don't be a fool any longer, Ab. The bloodshed and the bitterness have done enough hurt. I know you love home, and want to go back there. Your wife is waiting for you. This is your chance, Ab. I'll meet you in Tucson. Don't fail me, and don't fail yourself.

Always,

Blade

He had scribbled the address of a Tucson hotel where Ab could get in touch with him. Weeks drifted by and he had almost given up hope. A Mexican, with trail dust powdery on his clothes, brought him Ab's answer one day at the hotel.

Ab stated first that he didn't trust the United States of America any more now than he did the day they blockaded the Confederacy. Ab trusted one person, and that was Blade. He agreed to meet Blade, alone, at the Patchee Wells. He named the date.

That same afternoon, Blade left Tucson, riding south and east. Ab had not promised to go to Tucson. He wanted to hear more about that pardon, and any conditions. If it all sounded good to him when Blade met him at Patchee Wells, he would accompany him north, where he'd make his peace with the government.

The ride into the badlands was hot and slow. For hours the land seemed changeless. The wind was like the breath of a blast furnace. But Blade Merrick had been deep in his memories, and most of them were pleasant. He was remembering when he and Ab were boys on the Virginia farm. It was no plantation with slaves — those huge, feudal estates were few enough all through the South; less than one fourth of the people in the

South owned slaves.

Blade had found Virginia too crowded, too sweet-smelling for his liking. He went west, met a girl named Mary Beth and married her. When the war broke out he took Mary Beth to Dallas and joined a company of Texas volunteers. He had belonged to the Arizona-New Mexico territory, and the war was not his. But the anger against outside oppression was bred into him.

He had met Ab in Tennessee. It was the first time he'd seen his younger brother in over ten years. They had a week together. Blade was a sergeant and young Ab was a captain. Ab swore he'd move heaven and the Confederate capital to get Blade a commission. The next Blade heard, Ab had been taken prisoner.

He hadn't seen Ab again. After the war he heard that Ab had escaped the Yankee prison and made his way to the Mexican border. Ab had left a wife and a farm in Virginia, but was afraid to return.

Then the Federal government had

agreed to a full pardon.

Ab had had a chance at happiness right within his reach for the first time in ten years. Then somebody killed him at Patchee Wells and left his body to the ants.

Blade had covered every inch of the water hole. He figured how it must have been. Ab had been at Patchee Wells waiting for him. Three men had ridden in, and Ab, mistrustful, had grabbed his horse and hidden in the mesquite.

There were tracks, heel prints around the spring. Somebody had lain long, drinking, with his face in the pool. A man had smoked cigarettes. One of them had read a sign, or heard the slightest flicker of sound. They had dragged Ab out, gunned him down, ripped off his shirt and boots. They had ridden away then, going fast, and heading south.

That had been a month ago.

Merrick had tracked those men for three days and lost them in rock croppings far to the south. They'd known he was on their trail by then, and they moved on the slate stones, picking up their feet, but hurrying.

He had made his way back to Fort Ambush. He had questioned everyone about men headed south. Once he had worked; now he did nothing but hunt, obsessed with his hunting.

Something about these three men had filled him with the urgent fever to kill, the moment he saw them beside the burning wagon.

At first, the sight of the woman with the three hardcases had misled him. Then he learned that they'd picked up the pilgrims on the trail just a few hours before they were ambushed. aiding to the water hole, he had baited the boy about the bank robbery a month ago at Tucson, but the kid was wily. He had played with the bait, spit it out.

He stood up slowly, looking down at the mound of earth covering his brother's body. He remembered the way he'd found him, the brutal, senseless slaying.

Blood throbbed in his temples. He

told himself to move slowly. Anger and instinctive, murderous hatred were not enough. He had to have proof.

He tried to walk away from it. Hatred like this seared out a man's insides.

# 8

WHEN he heard the woman scream he spun around and ran up the incline. He had been away for only a few minutes; it didn't make sense that there'd been time for anything to happen in the camp. Perhaps her husband had died. He didn't think so. It wasn't that kind of screaming.

He drew his gun as he ran.

Perch Fisher still had her in his arms when Merrick came over the lip of land and raced down the incline toward the wagon. Her head was back and her hair flailed like flames in the wind.

Perch had one arm about her waist and a hand caught in the front of her dress. Her hands were free and she was clawing at him. Perch didn't even know she was striking him, scratching or clawing at his eyes. He knew only one thing, he had her body close against his body.

Merrick spun the gun around, catching it by the barrel to use as a club. But the Clintons were around the pool before he could reach the wagon.

Old Clinton reached across Fisher's shoulder, caught two fingers in his nostrils and yanked backwards. Perch screamed gutturally and fell back. Billy Clinton pinioned the man's arms at his side.

The girl staggered and toppled against the wagon, breathing wildly, staring at Perch and the Clintons.

"Christ," Perch yelled. "Christ, don't stop me!"

The Clintons were wrestling him toward the overhang.

"Next time I'll yank your head plumb off, boy," Hardhead Charley told him.

"Did you ever see a body like that, Charley?" Perch raged, struggling as they danced him along.

"Ain't you got troubles enough without spoilin' that dyin' man's woman?" Clinton shouted into his ear.

"Spoiling?" Perch was yelling, his voice quavering. "That's what's the matter now, for God's sake. She's spoiling. She needs a man. Let me go, for Christ's sake!"

They fought him to the overhang. Suddenly Clinton caught Perch in a bear hug, lifted his two hundred pounds off the ground, spun him around three times and hurled him with all his strength against the wall under the overhang.

Perch struck against the wall, flat, and the sound was like a goatskin tight with water dropped on stones. The breath was slammed out of him, but he came up on his knees crying and yelling. "Get out of my way, Charley. Get out of my way."

Clinton stepped forward and kicked Perch in the throat. He gasped, sobbing for air, and sprawled forward on the ground.

Across the pool at the wagon, Valerie was pressed back against the wheel, breathless. Her green eyes were swimming in tears.

Suddenly her head went back and laughter poured from her mouth, raging and spilling like water in a flash flood.

Merrick stared at her. The sound of her crazy laughter filled the sump, spilled out of it, spinning and racing in the afternoon silence.

He stepped forward. It had to come out of her. He thought bitterly, she was a woman who put everything she was into everything she did. When she had hysterics, she had them like no other woman ever had.

In the midst of her raging laughter the sobs would build and break. She had her head back, staring straight into the cloudless sky. Her mouth was pulled open with her sobbing and laughing. The sound vibrated in everything, seeming to congeal in the pit of Merrick's stomach and boil there.

Perch Fisher was sprawled on the ground, but both the Clintons had turned their backs on him and were staring open-mouthed at the laughing woman.

Merrick stepped forward. He brought the back of his hand across her face, hard.

She half fell under the impact. She pulled herself back up then, one last sob gulped back into her throat.

He stared at the livid marks of his hand against her cheek. Her eyes were wild, but the swirling shadows were dying in them.

She kept her gaze locked on his face. Her cheek muscles were rigid and her color was a paleness of death. She whimpered once, then her breathing quieted. She closed her lips and sagged against the wagon wheel, still watching him.

He heard footsteps behind him, turned. He was aware he still carried the gun and was holding it by the barrel.

"You won't need that on me," Hardhead Charley said. He nodded toward the gun. Merrick shoved it back into his holster. Clinton let his gaze move to the girl crouched on the blanket beside the wagon. "Though it wouldn't take much to make me as loco as Perch."

Merrick exhaled, did not answer. He didn't look at Valerie Butler, either. This was a strange land out here, and it hadn't taken him fifteen years to learn that. Women in the territories were revered, put on a pedestal and regarded as the Puritans regarded their women. But this was a hot land. Women were scarce. Sometimes it got so that ten thousand head of cattle, a pure vein of gold, a hundred square miles of ranchland didn't mean much. A man got a hunger that only a woman and violence could appease.

"What happened to him," Clinton said after a moment, "is that the woman called one of us over here to look at her husband. Perch came. Husband was all right. Perch dug around in the wagon, found some alcohol in a medicine bottle. He went back over there, drank it. You can't blame the alcohol entirely though. He's had his eye on her since the first minute he saw her."

Merrick looked at the wounded husband, sprawled on the blanket. He shook his head.

"The wonder is," Clinton said, also

looking at Jeff Butler, "that he ain't had her taken away from him long before this."

Merrick did not answer.

Perch called to Clinton. The huge old pirate went back around the water hole to the overhang. Perch said something Merrick could not hear. Clinton nodded and squatted against the wall.

About twenty feet around the pool from the wagon and directly across the water from the overhang where the Clintons were, was a ten-foot boulder. Merrick carried a blanket from the wagon and staked out the boulder for his own. The boulder gave him a wall to put his back against. He fought better that way when he was crowded.

He sat down with his back against the boulder. He wanted a cigarette, but when he lit one, he found it tasteless. He ground it out. There was only one thing wrong with him. He could feel the gaze of Valerie Butler on him from one point of this strange triangle, and from the other point, the Clintons and Perch Fisher were watching him and whispering. The Clintons were bad enough, but having that girl there, a torment just out of reach, another man's wife, that was worse.

He thought about Mary Beth, remembering the goodness and the excitement of her, and then recalling in anguish the way she had died six years ago. There hadn't been any other women after Mary Beth was killed. There never would be. The hurt had gone too deep. For a long time there had been madness that had taken her place.

He stared at the men across the pool. He would be all right, once he got out of here. If they made it to San Carlos, the Butler woman and her husband could go their way. He'd be all right again, left alone with his loneliness.

His mouth twisted into an acid smile. *What makes you think you'll ever get south to San Carlos? What makes you think those three men can't take your wagon and horses away from you? What are the odds that you won't end up dead right here at Patchee Wells, the way Ab*

99

*died?* Three men had ridden into this watering place and left Ab dead. Three men stared at him across that pool right now. Hardhead Charley Clinton had considered killing him within the first five minutes, back there in the valley. He must have gone over it a hundred times by now.

He shook his head. Even if they killed him, they would not get far. Those Apaches would be looking for them, soon. The trail led clearly from the valley to these Wells.

He shivered. His gaze pulled around again to Valerie Butler, the smooth skin of her face and throat, the full ripe body, ready for living. What a hell of a thing if the Apaches got her.

Perch was a gentlemanly choice, as against the warriors in that raiding party.

He cursed. No matter where he tried to take his thoughts, they came back to the Apaches, and what they could do to a woman. *It's hell, Mary Beth,* he thought. *It's a grim hot hell when you can't forget.*

"Mr. Merrick." The girl was kneeling over her husband. Her voice was frantic.

Merrick sprang to his feet, aware the men across the pool had stopped whispering and were watching him. He walked around the pool, for a moment caught by the reflections in it.

She looked up at him.

"Fever," she said. "He's burning up."

He knelt beside her, laid his hand over Butler's forehead. His fever was high, the heat penetrating Merrick's palm. Butler whimpered and twisted away from him.

"This is it," Merrick said to the girl across her husband. "This is the bad time. Either this fever will burn the poison out of him or — " He did not finish it.

She held his gaze levelly. Her face paled just slightly and she bit at her underlip. She did not say anything. He could see the marks of his fingers fading on her cheeks. A small desert animal skittered through the mesquite. The horses nickered from the grass clump.

101

He walked to the wagon, turned back the rear flaps. Inside were boxes, piled high, and they awaited them in San Carlos. He found the drug he wanted, returned to Butler. He held his head in his hand, forced the liquid between his lips.

"One thing we can fight," Merrick told her with a wry smile, "is fever."

"I — want to thank you for all you've done."

Mouth twisted into a bitter smile, he stared at her.

She colored slightly, touched her cheek with the backs of her fingers. "For everything," she told him.

He exhaled. One thing, those marks were fading. He would not have to go on looking at them. He got up, aware she was watching him, and replaced the medicine in the wagon. He turned then, glancing at her, walked toward the boulder he'd staked out as his own.

"Mr. Merrick."

He returned to the blanket.

"We're in your debt."

"Don't thank me. We're not out of this yet."

"But you stopped for us. You should be on your way somewhere — and it worries you."

"Nothing pressing. A fever epidemic at San Carlos. They should have had these drugs a week ago — couple days' delay won't matter much."

"I'm sorry . . . Is there someone there you care for very much?"

His mouth tightened. "There's no one I care for — anywhere."

"You're — not married?"

"I was."

"No woman ever left a man like you, Mr. Merrick."

"I don't know. Maybe she would have. She died before she got a chance." He breathed deeply. "Seems when I think back she hadn't even time to make up her mind about me one way or the other."

"I am sorry. I can understand now why you look so — unhappy."

"I'm just naturally a sour-looking cuss."

"No. It hurts deeply to lose the one you love."

He nodded toward her husband between them. "He's going to be all right, Mrs. Butler."

"Yes." She felt his forehead. The fever had not yet subsided. "I'm sure he will be."

He shook his head tiredly, looking at her husband and then at Valerie. "It's none of my business. But what's a girl like you — and a man like him — doing out here? From your voice, I'd say you're from Georgia — "

"South Carolina." She looked at the backs of her hands. "We came out here after the war. If you weren't there — in the South, after the surrender — you can't know what it was like."

"I was there for a while. I got back out as quickly as I could."

She nodded. "That's the way it was with Jeff and . . . I met him after the war. The — man I'd loved — he was killed. Jeff was gay and charming — despite all the misery around us. And that's what I needed then — just to laugh."

"You should have stayed there, done your laughing in your own country.

She nodded. "We know that now. Jeff got along well — even with the people who overran our land after the war. He — can be very ingratiating when he wants to — or needs to."

"There are worse talents."

"We were married. We would have gotten along all right, even there. But Jeff was unhappy. He had fought all during the war. Despite the fact he was friendly with the Yankees after the surrender, he had been fighting for his freedom — and he had lost that. He was restless, too. And — well, he got deeper and deeper in debt."

"So he thought it would be easier out here?"

"There were all kinds of glowing stories, Mr. Merrick, about the land, the fortunes to be made in cattle. Jeff wasn't really running away. Not entirely. He was in debt, he was restless, but his family had owned a huge place before the war. It was gone. He wanted a sprawling piece of his own, like the old estates had been. He believed he could buy land cheaply out here, raise cattle — and find the freedom and peace he was looking for."

His eyes held hers levelly. "And you? What did you want?"

She spoke to the backs of her hands. "What I want now. What I always wanted — a home and a family. We were losing everything back there — even each other. I didn't believe it could be any worse out here."

His mouth pulled down.

"Nobody ever does."

"Yes. It was too terrible. Too lonely — and too brutal. We — didn't have enough money to begin with. We were beaten from the start. We sold out, bought a wagon, loaded it up and headed back east — and got lost."

The sun was gone; the sky was a saffron color. It was still an hour to full dark.

Merrick climbed the knoll, seeking

the highest spot near the water hole. He could not discern a moving thing on the plains around him. This did not satisfy him, but he figured they had until morning before the Apaches found them. Even if they'd already found the wagon tracks, they would not move in tonight.

His laugh was bitter. Good to tell himself that, anyway. A fine fairy story it was, too. The Apache struck at the moment most advantageous to him.

He walked down to the boulder telling himself this was a pleasant thought to live with through the night.

The Clintons and Perch Fisher were almost lost in the shadowed overhang.

Hardhead Charley's bass voice struck at him as he sank to his blanket.

"We could put a lot of miles between us and this place tonight. Push them horses, we might make Fort Ambush by noon tomorrow. We three vote to pull out of here."

Merrick kept his voice level.

"I told you when we would travel," he

said. He waited a moment. "I also told you where."

The only answer was a derisive laugh from Perch Fisher. Merrick stepped back, putting his shoulders against the boulder. He could not see Perch Fisher under that overhang, and he didn't trust him where he could see him.

He heard a footstep near him and turned, his hand striking the butt of his gun.

"It's me," Valerie Butler said. "Would you come up with me to Jeff?"

He followed her around the pool edge, and up the slight incline. Terrible how taut tension could draw you. Here he was breathing through his mouth, jumpy, his heart slugging.

She knelt beside her husband. She touched his forehead. "His fever has subsided," she said.

He felt Butler's forehead, found it cool, checked his pulse. It was stronger, and Butler's breathing was more regular, less ragged. *He's breathing a lot better than I am,* Merrick told himself.

"I'll get him some water," Valerie whispered.

He remained on his knees, watching her move through the deepening dusk to the water hole. Not even the dusk could conceal what she was. He saw her kneel beside the water, fill his canteen and return up the incline.

Merrick lifted Jeff Butler's head. Valerie held the canteen to his lips. Jeff accepted some of it, moistening his parched lips. Most of the water ran down his chin, splotching his shirt.

She sat back. She poured water into her hands, patted it across her eyes and forehead, letting the beads trickle down her cheeks. "Cool," she whispered. "It's so cool."

She pressed the canteen to her mouth and drank greedily. "First water I've had," she said, gasping for breath. "I hadn't — even thought about water."

She extended the canteen. Merrick shook his head.

"It's so sweet and good," she said, voice awed.

Merrick nodded. "Sweet clear water is scarce in this country. Lot of it has a coppery taste. Some has an alkali taste. This water is good. It's funny. You've been out here as long as I have, you can tell where water comes from, by its taste. No matter where I tasted this water, I'd know it came from Patchee Wells."

She took another deep drink from the canteen. Merrick stood up, watching her head tilt back, her hair fall away from her shoulders, her throat moving.

She sighed. "I'll always remember the taste of this water, too," she said. Her voice was soft.

"Yes." His voice was chilled. "It's good water."

He turned and walked away.

"Mr. Merrick?"

He glanced over his shoulder. Why didn't she let him alone? Did she really think he was any less human than Perch Fisher? Wasn't he worse, because he didn't need medicinal alcohol to start his pulses pounding? A man can stand only so much loneliness — so little loneliness.

"Yes?"

"I heard — the Clintons asking you to take them to Fort Ambush."

"Yes."

"When can we travel?"

"As soon as your husband can be moved."

"You will take us — to Fort Ambush?"

He breathed deeply. "No. You heard them, then you heard me tell them I wouldn't."

"I beg you. Please. We were on our way to Tucson. We — we're so far from there now — I don't think we could make it — not from San Carlos."

"I'm sorry. You could head east from San Carlos — across New Mexico to Texas."

"We've friends in Tucson, Mr. Merrick. They'd help us. We've no money. We lost everything when the wagon burned."

"I can't turn back."

She reached out her hand toward him. He looked at her hand, lifted his gaze to her face. His mouth twisted.

"All I want," she whispered, "Is a

chance to get Jeff back east. We'd have a chance there — and we don't have any in this terrible, lawless place."

His gaze held hers for a moment. At last he said, "I'll fix some grub. You — you'll feel better after you've had something to eat."

# 9

THE night came on cool and wind-touched. It deepened all the shadows about the water hole. The sky was the impenetrable black of a bottomless void. As the wind rose, it keened around the boulders, cried in the lost, dark places. It gave movement to immobile things, and brushed a limb against your face where no limb ought to reach. You might feel a man standing close at your shoulder, and by the time you heeled around, you knew it wasn't a man at all, it was the wind, lonely and cold.

Merrick found himself straining to listen in those moments when the wind died. Somewhere in the dark there was a lonely cry, and no matter how long you'd been out here, sometimes it was hard to convince yourself it was the crying of the wind.

He had built fire enough to warm beans, sidemeat and coffee. Valerie sat with them under the overhang. The fire flickered in their faces, was reflected in their eyes. They drank coffee from tin cups.

Merrick poured his fifth cup, drank it black. He had to stay awake. He couldn't remember ever having been so tired. The hatred that had chewed at him all day had squeezed out his strength. The fact that if he slept he would never wake up worked against him, too. His nerves were drawn taut, and having Valerie beside him in the firelight, seeing the way Billy and Perch licked at her with their eyes, didn't help any either.

Valerie was listening to the cry in the wind. Her voice was hollow. "You get so you wish for any sound," she said. "Because except for the wind there isn't anything." She shivered. "I hate it. I don't see how anyone would willingly stay out here."

Hardhead Charley Clinton's laugh rattled under the overhang. "Why, ma'am, loneliness ain't the worst thing that can happen to a man."

Merrick's laugh was sharp and cold. He stared at Clinton beside him in the flickering firelight.

"No," he said. "There's always the hang-rope."

Though Merrick expected another response, Clinton only laughed again, louder.

"I'm not a man as would lie to you, Merrick. I've had myself some brushes with the law. Like I was telling the little lady, there's been many times when I welcomed a lonely spot like this where I could hide."

"How about this one?" Merrick said. "You ever hide out here?"

He heard Billy Clinton's lazy laugh. "I bet every one of us has had a turn, Merrick, telling you we didn't know this place. What's the matter? You own it or something?"

"No. I don't own it."

Clinton laughed again. "Seems to me this afternoon I seen a look in your face that said right plain you don't even like this place."

"I could live without it."

"So could we," Billy said across the fire. "So quit pushing it, Merrick."

Merrick looked at them, slowly. "My brother was killed here."

"Say, I'm mighty saddened to hear a thing like that," Clinton said.

"Are you?"

"I said I was. I know what a man's kin means to him. My boy Billy, there. He's all I got. Whatever I do, on whatever side of the law I am, I do it so I can give my boy Billy better than I ever had."

Merrick's voice remained expressionless. "Whoever killed my brother never gave him a chance. Shot him in the back. Then filled him with lead. It was a willful, senseless killing."

"Lots of killings don't make sense when you look back on them," Clinton said.

Merrick was aware that Perch Fisher had straightened up against the wall. His eyes did not blink as he watched Merrick.

Beside him, Valerie had forgotten her coffee, had almost forgotten to breathe.

"They ripped off his boots, and his shirt — left him lying in the sun."

"Sounds like Indians," Clinton said.

"After a man's dead, he don't care much where he's laid out, is the way I look at it," Billy Clinton said.

"It wasn't Indians." Merrick ignored Billy. "They would have robbed him."

Clinton swigged down a gulp of coffee, then poured himself another cup, watching the steam.

"You've had a rugged time, Merrick. A man would have to be mighty heartless to deny that. But let me tell you, Charley Clinton never had it easy. I took to living by the gun. I admit that to you people. But I never done it from choice. It was forced on me — back when my boy Billy was just a lad. I had steaded me some land, lived on it with my woman and my boy. When they deprived me of my lands, I figured somebody had to pay for it." He slapped his leg and laughed. "And I been making them pay for it ever since.

Perch and my Billy and me. We learned from them stinkin' Apaches. We strike and we run. Ain't that right, Perch?"

"We take what we want, all right." Perch was staring at Valerie.

"We hit these badlands when we have to. And we cross the border. But living ain't as good down that way, and my boy Billy gets kind of restless down there. That's why we're heading north again."

As he talked, his voice filling the darkness around the sump, Merrick stared at the big man thinking that his ancestors had roamed the north seas, plundering and pillaging. Clinton was a pirate, too, roving the wastelands and striking at the towns.

"I was cheated. Cheated out of my lands. My woman died. But I'm going to have myself a stake one of these days. A big stake. The name of Clinton will be respected in the towns."

"They already respect my name in the towns," Billy said. He laughed.

"Son, you ain't going to have to shoot your way into town — and out of them.

I still mean to buy lands, and raise cattle. My boy is going to be a big man in this territory — respected, admired — "

Perch laughed. "I'm gettin' sick of your jawing, Hardhead. I heard a lot of versions about your ranching days. Heard you used the running-iron mighty free — even in your most honest days."

Clinton nodded. "We all did. When we rounded-up, we couldn't stop to count out a man's strays. I reckon I lost as many as I branded for my own."

"I doubt it." Perch's laugh was derisive. "That just don't sound like you, Hardhead."

Clinton's voice was wounded, cold. "A man has got to look out for hisself — and his own."

Perch was watching Valerie, pleased with the ribbing he was giving old Clinton. "You ever shoot a man in the back, Hardhead, when he stayed overnight at your place?"

Clinton said "A man looks after his own."

Perch sniggered. "Why, don't take

offense, Hardhead. It's just that I say you were as treacherous and ornery during them ranching days as you are right now." He gave the old man a mocking nod of the head. "No offense intended, of course."

Clinton turned, looking at Merrick with a false smile. "Merrick, I have admired you much today. *Mucho*, like they say down south of the border. You're the sort of *hombre* what makes a fine friend and a *muy malo* man to have for an enemy. I know we have had some things to disagree about today, but in the long run, there's one thing both of us are."

Merrick waited.

"Yes sir, I will say that we both are reasonable men. You figure yourself a reasonable man, Merrick?"

Merrick stared at him, waiting.

Clinton laughed falsely again. "Why, sure goodbilly hell you do. That's why I can talk to you reasonable. Like a reasonable man."

Clinton waited, but Merrick did not

say anything. "Its about gettin' a fast running start toward Fort Ambush — "

"I already told you."

"Wait now. Wait. Hear me out. The boys and me understand you got a real burr under your tail to get down there to San Carlos. We figure maybe there's money in it for you — something like that. But I never met a man in my life that wouldn't change his plans if the price was right. You found that to be true, Merrick — I mean if the man was reasonable?"

"I reckon every man's got his price."

"Well now, there you are. To show you we are friendly, we'll tell you right out — them saddle bags are poked full of spending money. Yes sir, we got three bags full of money."

"Yours?" Merrick's smile was bland. The look on Clinton's face matched his. He slapped his leg and laughed. "It is now. And that's what the boys and me talked over. We're willing to offer you a firm one thousand dollars in Federal money to turn them horses around — tonight — and hightail it north to Fort Ambush."

"A thousand dollars," Merrick said.

"That's right. A whale of a lot more'n you'd make in a year going the other way. True?"

Merrick nodded. "A thousand dollars would buy a lot of beefsteak."

Clinton's voice chilled, fell away. "Take it, Merrick. Do yourself a favor and take it."

Merrick was watching Billy and Perch across the fire. Billy's face was twisted with a secretive grin. Perch was watching him, contempt flaring his nostrils slightly.

"You, Billy. And Perch. You willing for me to share in that money?"

Billy laughed. "Sure. Take it."

Perch shrugged. "Why not?"

Valerie spoke for the first time. "Please."

Clinton said, "You take the money, Merrick. Now, we got to stay reasonable. You know what's in our minds. We mean to take them horses and head north."

"And me — I'm gettin' sick of jawing about it," Perch said. "You want the thousand, you take it, and we head north. Take it, mister, because you ain't got much choice."

"Turn back — and stay alive," Billy said. "It's real simple."

Merrick's voice was level. "Not quite. You see, there's an epidemic down there in San Carlos."

Perch laughed. "Maybe you don't realize it, mister. There's an epidemic right here — and you're about to die from it."

Clinton's curse stopped Perch. "Now listen to me, Merrick. We can still stay friendly about this thing. The boys and me — we come up from the south. Between here and San Carlos there ain't nothing but godforsaken country and hostiles. Now if we headed north, in less than a day we might meet a patrol from Fort Ambush if we lathered them horses. It don't make sense any way at all to go south. Nobody would hold it against you if you turned back — nobody expects you to get killed to get medicine down to that mission."

"Stop talking about it, Hardhead." Perch leaned forward. "Tell him. We're heading out of here before morning. Going north — with him, or without him."

"You race that wagon north," Merrick said. "Two things are sure to happen. You'll be sure to kill that man down there — he'd bleed to death. The other thing is that those same Apaches would trail you, and that would mean getting this woman killed . . . and it still don't mean you'd make it."

Perch snorted his derision. "Man, you really worry about things, don't you? Sick people got to have medicine. A man might bleed. Oh, boy, what you got is Southern honor."

"Kinda like a sickness," Billy said. "A man could die with it. You ever see a man die with that Southern honor sickness, Perch?"

"Hell, I seen them rebel nogoods die in packs. Man, I marched through that country once. The roads are terrible. Them rebels call it a highway — and up home we'd call it a pig track."

Billy shook his head. "Me? I heard so much about them big plantations. Most of them Southern trash I saw was living on grits and sidemeat."

"Listen," Perch said. "Whilst we was marching, we kept hearing about Southern hams. Southern hams. Hell, we stole a few. Now, I ain't lying to you, it was so full of fat you couldn't cook it."

"Sure," Billy said. "They ain't got nothing else, so they sit around telling each other they got Southern honor. So, why don't you get smart, Merrick? You been out here long enough to get some sense. Take a thousand dollars and let's get out of here."

Merrick poured the dregs from his coffee cup. He felt Valerie's eyes on him. He did not look at her. He kicked sand into the fire so it sputtered and died.

Darkness shrouded them. It flooded in, drowning out everything. While it was black dark, Merrick got to his feet and moved away from the overhang.

"Merrick?" Clinton's deep voice stabbed after him in the darkness.

Leaning against a boulder, Merrick answered him.

"I want no trouble with you, Merrick," Clinton said.

"That's fine."

"But I better tell you. I'll kill you and take them horses if that's the only way I can get to Fort Ambush. You think that over."

"I want you three to sleep well, too, Clinton," Blade said. "So think about me across that pool. I'll be there when you come to take that wagon."

He moved away in the darkness. He heard Valerie get up and hurry through the darkness to the gray blotch that was the wagon. He could hear the rustle of her skirts in the silence.

There was no movement from the overhang. He flopped down on his blanket, mouth twisted. Nobody would get much rest tonight. If they slept at all up there, it would be the sleep of watchful men.

# 10

"MERRICK . . . Blade."

He pulled up against the boulder. She was standing near him. She was only a dim outline in the darkness, but the soft feminine fragrance of her was midday clear. He felt tense. She brought danger with her. It was different from the danger of the men across the pool, but it was none the less potent.

Above the rim of the sump he saw the stars were beginning to show. The first darkness was clearing away and the sky seemed to melt as the stars appeared, making each separate planet seem to burn bright and singly, just out of reach.

The cry of the wind was faint. The men across the pool seemed far away. He wondered if for a moment he had fallen into a light sleeping state. He had to watch that. At the moment he was dazed, and only the woman's nearness had reality.

The men across the pool were wide awake. They had heard Valerie's whisper.

"The woman with you again, Merrick?" Clinton called. "How's her man going to take that?"

"Bleeding to death ain't the only way for a man to die," Perch said.

Young Billy laughed. "What is it you got, Merrick, that I don't have?"

Perch laughed. "Why, it ain't that a-tall, Billy-boy. What he's got is that old Southern honor. Man's nothing but honor and the woman trusts him. It's plumb a caution the way she has come to rely on Blade Merrick."

"That's a living fact," Billy said.

Their taunting voices rode across the pool.

Perch swore. "Why, it's like as though good-looking Mrs. Butler don't trust us at all — us that tried to keep her alive and away from the Injuns."

Clinton's voice had no laughter in it,

but the taunt barbed it. "Let her fool around with him, and the Injuns *will* get her."

"She'll know who to trust," Perch said. But it's going to be too late when the Injuns get their hands in that pretty mess of red hair."

Billy emitted a mock moan. "Oh, what a sin it would be to waste anything like that on Injuns."

The three men laughed. Merrick strained to hear their movement. It seemed to him they must be crouched at the very rim of the overhang, staring down at the boulder.

He heard the affection in old Clinton's voice. "Billy, you're growing into a right fine man. I'm proud of you. You got taste in women, boy," Clinton said into the silence.

Blade kept his voice low. "They'd like to get me to answer them," he said. "They'd take a shot at me if they were sure the first would get me."

"Jeff — is awake."

"Is he feeling better?"

"Yes. His fever is gone." She bent toward him, keeping her voice low. He could smell the woman — fragrance of her hair and her body. The fresh clean smell assailed him, and he wanted to tell her to get away from him, to stay away. She'd been out here long enough to know how scarce women were. God knew this was worse. He admitted it was different. He had been near women in the towns, at the army posts — few as they were, he could have been with some of them if he had wanted to. But it looked as though hell was playing a dirty trick on him. All his desire was congealed and focused on this woman. And she didn't have sense enough to stay away from him.

"You've saved his life," she whispered. "I never met a better man than you, Blade."

*Sure,* he thought. *What a fool you are.* He looked at her, yearning in the darkness.

"You're a gentleman. I haven't met many like you out here."

He sighed, thinking, *And I haven't*

130

*met any like you.* Then he warned himself that she could be here because she wanted just what the Clintons wanted — to turn that wagon north to Fort Ambush.

"I'm glad your husband's better."

"He sent me over," she said. "He's awake, and feeling better. He wants to talk to you."

"I want to thank you," Butler said when Merrick hunkered down beside his blanket.

He extended his slender hand. Blade took it. There were no calluses on Butler's palm. If he had worked for his woman since he came out here, he must have done it in saloons, over gambling tables. Hell, he told himself, forget it. It's none of your business, and you got worries enough. She chose this man. Let her live with him.

He frowned. Would he be so critical of her husband if he was not all ripped up about the woman?

"It's all right." His voice was brusque.

"You'd do as much for me."

"That's it, old buddy. I don't know. You see, Val told me about that bullet. It was deep. She said you took it out like you were digging for precious metal."

"I don't know too much about a man's insides. I probe careful because I don't want to open something I can't close." Blade wished Jeff Butler would get to the point. He found himself disliking even the young fellow's voice. Funny how you could hate a man just because he had something you wanted, so that even his voice fretted and angered you. Jefferson Calhoun Butler had a Carolina drawl that was almost a whine.

And Valerie's skirts rustled as she knelt by Jeff, across from him. The wind filled his nostrils with that perfume that wasn't perfume at all, but *her.*

Jeff said, "Well, you saved my life. I'm glad you saw fit to be so careful."

"How do you feel now?"

"Like you left your right hand in my side."

"It'll be better. Bound to be sore for

a while. If you don't bleed any more, you'll make it."

"That's what I want to talk to you about." Jeff's whine drew out each word so that Merrick flinched at the sound.

"Yeah?"

"I guess I don't have to tell you in a lot of words, Merrick. I was never meant for this country. Sure, I thought I was. Val and I — we talked ourselves into it. Back home, I guess I'd be as good as the next man."

"Sure." Merrick glanced at Valerie, wondering what had first attracted her to this man. There wasn't much laughter in a man as weak as this one.

"I mean, I went all through the war. I was on the general's staff, sure. But we went into the fighting."

"I know."

"Sometimes the fighting came up to us. I never ran away from it. After the war, I went back home, and I felt I was as good as the next man. You know? I don't feel that way out here. There's too much you got to know, just to stay alive." He tried to laugh, but his voice quavered. "Hell, I thought I knew south from north — and east from west. But once Val and I got in that wagon — I even lost my sense of direction."

"It happens. All the time."

"I hate to depend on another man. But Val and I talked it over. We need help. Bad. She told me how Clinton and the other two threatened you."

He glanced up at Valerie. "She's filled you in with everything that's happened, eh?"

"I woke up a while ago." The drawling whine sawed at Merrick's taut-drawn nerves. "I heard you people talking up there. When Val came back, I asked her about it. Now, I — I know you're going to do what's best — for all of us — eh, Merrick?"

Merrick stared at Butler a moment, lifted his gaze to Valerie. Even in the darkness she could not meet his gaze. He heard the low-toned conversation from the overhang, the distant cry of the wind. Somewhere in the wastes a coyote bayed.

"I don't know," he said at last. He stood up. He didn't want to hear the man whine and beg, not in front of the woman. At the moment all he wanted was to escape both of them. "I reckon I'll do what I have to."

"Sure. Sure."

"A man's got to live with himself."

He walked away down the incline, hearing the soft whisper of the water running out of the well, falling on a stone. He could hear the muted conversation of the Clintons, but he paid no attention to it.

He walked quietly, thinking it over, the man and his woman that were nothing to him, and the way he would remember her every night as long as he lived.

His grin was acrid. It happened that way sometimes. Hard, sudden and complete. And when it hit you, it was too bad. You could run away from it, but you couldn't stay in the same world with it . . . not and do nothing about it.

He shook his head, hating his thoughts.

Jeff Butler had so little now; it was almost as if the woman were his last reservoir of strength — take her away, and what was left of him?

He heard the whisper of sound behind him. He slowed, feeling panic only because he knew it was Valerie.

"Could I talk to you — just a minute?"

"If it's about heading north, I can't do it."

"No. It's about — Jeff." Her voice dropped.

He caught his breath. *Good God*, he thought, *don't apologize. Whatever you do, don't apologize for him.*

"He's sick." she said. "The bullet — the loss of blood. Really, he's very charming, and not afraid. Why, like he said, he went all through the war."

"He seems a good fellow."

"No. He was whining. I saw you — the way you withdrew."

"He's bad hurt."

"But there's more than that, and you know it. He's frightened — he's almost more afraid of living than — than of dying from that wound."

"A man gets down low, he can't help how he feels."

"It'll be worse. He heard what those men think of Southerners — he heard them trying to rile you into fighting. If they start on him — " She shuddered, standing close to him in the darkness. "You — you're from Virginia. You're one of us. Won't you try to help him?"

He spread his hands. "What could I do?"

"Don't let him be afraid — not in front of them."

"You might as well know — because a man is from Carolina or Virginia doesn't mean he's either brave or a coward. Like all places — there are both. A man is smart to know when to be scared."

"But — " her voice faltered — "fear is paralyzing him — and that's not smart."

"No." His voice was cold. "You're right. It ain't smart to be scared all the time."

# 11

SHE went away from him, up the incline to the wagon. Merrick heard her moving around for some minutes and then could hear her lie down beside her husband.

He shivered with something more than the cold in the wind. He scooped out a place for his hipbone under the roll of the boulder and lay down on his blanket.

The horses were restless in the grass clump. He heard them blowing, pulling against their stakes. A small night animal slithered near him, and he heard the wind die, and the rustling of the trees as it rose again in the night.

The stars looked yellow and swollen, and the sky beyond them had paled, fading. He did not know how late it was but knew it did not matter. He could not sleep. He yawned, knowing he had never been more exhausted.

His eyelids were heavy. He felt drowsy, almost as if he had been drugged. The coffee had not helped much. He'd been afraid it would not. It had been served up with tension and hatreds that you could almost touch.

Lying on his side, he strained his eyes, starring at the depression beneath the overhanging boulder across the pool. Soon, enough moonlight and starlight would fade the darkness to gray, but at the moment he could not see them over there.

He propped his head on his arm. Clinton had warned him clearly enough. They meant to take the wagon and the horses and move out tonight. They would not even hesitate to kill him if he opposed them. He wondered if they would bother to take Valerie and Jeff Butler with them. It was certain that neither Billy nor Perch would want to leave her here. No. They'd take her if they ran before dawn, but the odds were they'd leave her husband and him dead — if they could get away with it.

He glanced at the sky, needing just a little more light under that overhang. He had to see them moving. They had plotted for hours. Whatever their plan was, it should now be well-discussed.

He sighed. Clinton had a neat purpose in warning him that he could expect them during the night. It had not been to prepare him. They knew he waited. Clinton wanted him to worry about *when* it would happen.

He heard Valerie and Jeff whispering in the darkness. He let his thoughts touch her because there was more pleasure, if no less danger, in thinking about her.

He had no idea how long he'd lain there when he heard the first whisper of movement.

The gray starlight had touched the depression beneath the overhang where the Clintons were. This light on the three shadowy forms over there, along with his own fatigue, had lulled him.

He waited, pressed against the boulder, tense. The sound was louder now, the

140

noise a mouse might make, or a man moving across the crust of the sand.

He lifted his head, stared at the wagon. He could see the outlines of Valerie and Jeff over there. He moved his gaze around. The hell of it was there were still three forms under that overhang . . . or there appeared to be.

For a moment he thought it might be an Apache. If this were true, they'd lose the horses and he ought to call out to Clinton for help.

But he did not call out. He could not delay any longer. He got to his knees, letting the blanket fall away from him. He kicked his boot free.

There was the sound of a footstep in the darkness to his right around the boulder. The sound died and silence followed, as if someone held his breath.

Merrick worked his gun free of its holster. Thumbing back the hammer, he got to his knees, pressing close against the boulder, slithering cautiously. He took two steps, paused.

He glanced across the pool at the

overhang. They could be waiting for him to step away from the shadow of the boulder, to show himself in the moonlight.

There was no movement under the overhang. Still, he had the nagging sense of wrong in this. He pressed himself back into the shadowed dark of the boulder.

A horse pawed the earth, so that part of it was all right: the horses hadn't been stolen yet. The wind chose this moment to die away. Merrick closed his mouth, forcing himself to breathe through his nose. The splash of water on the stone inside the pool seemed exaggeratedly loud. It was as if it were the regular heartbeat of this place.

Sweat broke out across his forehead. It was too quiet, an unnatural tension, drawing tighter and tighter like a wire that's going to snap. The Butlers asleep beside the wagon. The sound of the water dropping. The three dark forms that might be the Clintons, or else blankets piled on stones to look like them. The sky was lightening. He had no idea what time it was, only that it was hours until daybreak; the sky would darken over completely again before dawn. He waited, feeling the chill touch of the wind on his sweated face.

The sound of a footstep on the alkali crust was repeated; brush crackled. Some of the tension went out of Merrick and he almost laughed. The danger wasn't lessened, but there was no longer any doubt. They were begging him to investigate that noise. It was as if they whispered across the darkness, *Step out there, Merrick. Please. Come on out where we can see you.*

He moved cautiously to the left of the boulder, away from the sound of the brush and the footsteps. He pressed his body against the boulder, sliding around it.

In the darkness of the boulder, he crouched and stared through the gloom.

The set-up hit him with the impact of a fist. It rocked him on his heels to think they believed he'd fall for such a simple plot. A few yards away from him, across a clearing, Billy Clinton stood near a mesquite bush. In his right hand Billy had his gun, in the other he held a forked stick. He punched at the mesquite and it rattled faintly: the sound a man might make creeping up on his prey.

Perch was the joker in the trap — out there in the clearing; Billy was the bait. The plan was simple enough; catch Merrick in the space between them and cut him down in the crossfire.

He waited another moment, holding his breath. Perch was only a few feet from him, poised in the shadows, gun drawn, awaiting a signal from Billy. There was a chance the trap had another snapper — old Clinton could be the cincher, but there was not time to look for him. In a moment, Perch's instinct would warn him, or he'd hear Merrick breathing behind him.

Merrick twisted the gun, making a club of it. He braced himself and sprang toward the crouching Perch.

Clinton's warning yell came from across

the water hole. It rattled against the rocks.

"Look out, Perch! Look out behind you!"

Perch straightened, spinning around on his heel. He was fast, but not fast enough. He brought his gun upward but did not get to fire it. Driven by his anxiety, Merrick chopped down with the gun butt. He could feel the shock of the blow all the way to his shoulder. There was the sound of wood and metal against Perch's skull.

Perch uttered an exhaling sound of agony and crumpled at the knees, pitching toward Merrick.

Blade moved to his left, away from Perch's toppling body.

Across the clearing in the mesquite, Billy Clinton hurled the stick from him and turned toward them, firing in the darkness.

The bullet chipped stone from the boulder beside Blade's face. Billy ran toward him, into the clearing, ready to fire again.

Blade did not hurry it. He crouched slightly in the shadows, leveled his gun at Billy's hand-carved belt. He pressed off his shot coldly. The impact of the bullet caught Billy squarely in the chest, knocking him his own length backwards into the dirt.

Merrick waited. There was a faint sobbing cry from within the clearing. In the faint light he saw that Billy's gun had been knocked from his hand as he fell. It lay some feet from him.

Billy had landed on his back, turned slightly on his side. He did not move.

Merrick felt the sickness well up in him. It had nothing to do with the killing; that was self-defense. Maybe it was the kid's age, the way he had laughed, had tilted his hat.

"Blade! Merrick? Are you all right?"

He heard Valerie calling from the wagon. He hoped she had sense enough to stay where she was. Clinton was going to be firing at anything that moved.

Clinton yelled. "Billy? Billy-boy. You all right?"

The wind rose, and the night chill deepened around the water hole.

"Billy! Perch! Billy! Goddamm it, boy, answer me.

His gun ready, Merrick knelt and caught Perch by the collar. He dragged him around the boulder.

"Perch. That you, boy?"

Clinton's voice was frantic. He forgot himself enough to run out from beneath the overhang.

Merrick raised his gun.

"Hold it, Clinton. Right out there in the open where you are."

Clinton stopped as though he'd been poled. He held his gun at his side.

"You toss that gun away from you, Clinton," Merrick said.

"Billy?"

There was no answer. After a moment Clinton dropped the gun. He stood, swaying slightly, near the water hole.

Merrick dragged Perch around the rim of the pool.

"Stand quiet, Clinton. You make a move, you're tagged."

Clinton seemed not to hear him. He was staring at the opening between the wagon and the boulder. They'd set the trap out there, set it with Billy as the bait, laughing as they planned it because nothing could go wrong. They'd live forever, all three of them, and share the loot from their latest haul in a Tucson saloon.

Merrick moved to within three feet of Hardhead Charley Clinton. He released his hold on Perch's shirt collar and stepped back.

Clinton did not see him, or Perch. His craggy face was rigid. His eyes were distended, fixed on that open place between wagon and boulder. In a moment Billy had to saunter through there, hat rakish, thumb in his belt.

The sound was ripped from Clinton's throat.

"Billy!"

The wind was his answer; the wind, the silence, and the whisper of the water in the pool.

"Boy. Billy, boy!"

148

Clinton shook his head, said, "Ah-h-h." The pain was intolerable, and yet he was numb, beyond pain.

"Goddam it, Billy-boy. You hear me, Billy? You hear me? You answer me."

Clinton stepped toward that opening, going down the incline. He almost stepped on Perch's face.

Merrick's voice was rasping. "Hold it. Right there, Clinton."

Clinton stopped, but did not turn around. He sobbed, standing there, his big shoulders shaking. The noises from his mouth were animal sounds, full of grieving and loss. Billy was dead, and he had to believe it. Billy was never going to die and Billy was dead.

He turned slowly. Tears were running from his eyes. His nose was running and when his mouth moved, he slobbered. He looked down at Perch Fisher as though he had never seen him.

"My boy. My boy." He lifted his head, a pirate out of time and place. His mouth twisted. "My boy. I had nothing else. You've killed my boy.

149

I'm looking at you, Merrick. You killed my boy. God help you, Merrick. You'll never live — you'll never close your eyes again on this earth — not until I kill you . . . "

Merrick stood there with the whine of the wind loud through the rocks. A faint film of dust sifted across the pool. He heard Valerie Butler's sharp intake of breath from the shadow beside the wagon. He did not take his gaze from Clinton.

He saw Clinton's hand falter toward his holster, find it empty. Clinton moaned again.

He stared at Merrick across Perch's prostrate body. Then he pulled his gaze away. Merrick saw him find the gun where he'd dropped it, saw him quiver toward it, almost lunging toward it though Merrick stood with his own gun, waiting.

At last, Clinton quieted, pulled his gaze away from his gun.

Merrick knelt slowly, watching Clinton. He removed Perch's gun from its holster.

Clinton remained immobile.

Merrick backed up the incline, gathered the three rifles from beneath the overhang. He came back to where Clinton stood, gaze riveted on his gun on the ground.

Merrick said, "Take Perch up there to the overhang, Clinton. Do what you want to for him. He may die."

Clinton stared at him, bent down, caught Perch's collar, dragged him up the incline. Merrick gathered up the gun, went down to his boulder.

He heard Clinton pacing back and forth across the water hole. He walked to the clearing.

Merrick knelt beside Billy's body. The boy was dead. He found his gun, went slowly back to the sump.

Clinton was standing near the wagon. In another moment he would have made it to the boulder and the guns.

When he saw Merrick, Clinton swung around. His voice shook. "Butler, give me your gun. Give it to me. I'll kill him. I got to kill him or I can't go on living. Give me the gun."

Merrick moved near to Clinton. "Get back to your cage, Clinton. You tried a kill and it didn't work. You can thank God you're still walking around."

Clinton shrugged his shirt up on his shoulders, eyes locked upon Merrick, burning his face into his mind.

Merrick said, voice cold and dead, "In the morning you better bury your boy, Clinton, unless you want the buzzards helping the Apaches find you quicker than they will anyhow."

He heard Clinton moan, helpless and torn with inner rage. He turned his back on Clinton, walked down to his blanket. He was more tired than he had ever been in all his life before.

# 12

IN the darkest hour before daybreak, Merrick left the boulder, going quietly around it. He walked past Billy Clinton's body, twisted like something broken in the sand.

He went up on the highest point above the sump. The rocks crowded him and the wind whispered around them, a cold whisper of trouble and sudden death.

He searched the land with sleepless eyes. The ache in them extended to the crown of his head now. He rubbed them with the heel of his hands, turning slowly to search every point of the compass.

Nothing stirred out there. He didn't know what he expected to find at this hour. If the Indians had found the horses they would be gorging themselves on roasted meat. If that were true, they had found the tracks leading south to Patchee Wells. But it might be also true that the Apache might lie around on his full belly, spend a few more hours making medicine. But if they were feasting on roasted meat there should be a fire reflected in the darkness from the valley.

There was nothing out there. The silence pressed in upon him. Whatever the Apache was about, he was not going to learn it up here.

He went down the incline, untied the horses and led them down to the pool, let them drink. He saw Perch was sprawled on the ground at the lip of the overhang. Clinton had sworn he would not sleep, but his grief and anguish had overcome him. He was toppled back against the wall of the depression. He snored in his sleep.

Merrick led the horses to the wagon, backed them between the shafts, hitched them to the wagon.

"Are you leaving?"

He turned, finding Valerie standing at the corner of the wagon, watching him.

"Maybe. If your husband hasn't bled

too much during the night. If he feels well enough."

"Are you still going south?"

"I have all the guns."

"Not all of them."

"Would you shoot me?"

"I don't know. You should have taken Jeff's gun when you took the others."

He straightened the lines, checking them. His voice was level. "Thanks for warning me."

"Too late now, Mr. Merrick. Jeff and I talked it over last night. He won't give you his gun. You'll have to shoot him — like you did that boy."

"That *boy* missed me by inches. Was I supposed to stand there? You are just as dead, killed by a boy."

"I know you did what you had to do. You miss my point. I was trying to tell you, we were on your side. You were good to us; you saved Jeff's life. But this is different. This is our chance to get back home . . . "

"So you've thrown in with Clinton and Perch."

"We don't know yet. That's up to you. We know he has a lot of money. He is very anxious to go north. He wants to go south to San Carlos even less than Jeff and I do. If you force him to travel south, you'll have to fight him every step of the way."

He was bent over checking a horseshoe. He released the horse, straightened.

"That's where you're wrong. I'm not forcing anyone to go south with me. I told you people. *I'm* going south. If you want to go with me, fine. But it's up to you."

He heard her sharp intake of breath. "You'd leave them — or us, in this Indian country?"

"I'd hate it," he told her. "But as I said, it's your choice."

"I'm glad to see you for what you are. You're less than human."

He shrugged. "Maybe, Mrs. Butler. But it's a long ways to San Carlos, and there are Apaches — I'll have enough to do without battling the people riding with me."

She moved her hand upward from the folds of her dress. He saw the gleam of the long gun barrel.

"Put that thing down," he said.

"Stay where you are, Merrick. I've given this a lot of thought. If you think I won't shoot you, you just don't know how badly I want to get back east."

"Pull the trigger," he said.

"W-what?"

"You heard me. You're not going to shoot me unless you pull that trigger. And you're not getting these horses unless you kill me."

She breathed in deeply. He saw her brush at a lock of hair on her forehead.

"Don't try any tricks," she said.

"The tricks are up to you. Coming over here with a sweet, friendly tone and pulling a gun. Go on, shoot me. Then let's see you people get north past those Mescaleros."

"We — can try it."

"Sure you can. You tried it once before. Only there was one more of you than there is now — and Perch Fisher has a cracked skull this morning. Don't count much on him. And you've got a long run ahead of you in that wagon, and the rattling around is sure to start your husband to bleeding — so you can count him as dead — "

"Shut up!"

Her cry rang against the inner wall of the sump. Old Clinton came to his feet in the first thin rays of day light. He stared down at Valerie holding the gun on Merrick and roared.

"You just hold that, Miz Butler," he yelled. "I'm a-coming to take over."

Valerie turned to look at him. From the blanket Jeff yelled her name in warning. But it was too late.

Merrick sprang forward, grabbing her arm, twisting it and pulling her around between him and the running Clinton.

He wrested the gun from her hand, held it toward Clinton.

"All right, old man. Stop right there."

Clinton took three more long running steps before he was able to halt.

"Godamighty, woman, why didn't you watch him?"

Blade was more aware of the pressures of her body against him than of Clinton's swearing, or of Jeff Butler propped on his elbows watching them from the blanket. He would have sworn he could feel the frantic thudding of her heart, or perhaps it was just the echo of his own. He thrust her away from him.

She stumbled and fell on the blanket beside Jeff. He did not look at her. His mouth was pulled down in petulant anger.

In the shelter of the boulder where he'd spent most of the night, Merrick made a small fire, banked with stones. He heated coffee, fried biscuits and warmed meat.

By the time the smell of coffee had filled the sump, Clinton was watching him from the lip of the overhang.

Valerie had walked to the edge of the wagon.

He poured a cup of coffee. "Will you join me?"

She came around the pool slowly. She would not look at him.

"Don't feel badly," he said. "You did as well as any of them. Better. You got nearer to me than I would have let them get."

He handed her a cup of coffee, a tin plate of warm meat, beans and fried biscuits.

She drank the hot coffee and ate hungrily. Merrick watched her a moment, glanced up at Clinton. "Come down here and get a plate, Clinton."

Clinton came down around the pool.

"All right," Merrick said when he was ten feet from the fire, "you can hold that."

He placed a cup of coffee on a stone in front of Clinton, then put a plate of food beside it.

Clinton squatted beside the stone and began to eat. He did not say anything. Merrick saw that Clinton's eyes were red-rimmed, his face stark, pallid.

Perch stood up slowly, walked dazedly down to the pool. He sank down beside it, bathing his face and moaning.

Merrick set a plate of food and coffee near him. Perch turned, looking at the food. The sudden turn made his head pain, and he touched at his skull.

"Must have walked into something in your sleep last night," Merrick said.

Perch touched his holster, found it empty. His face went blank and he paled beneath his sunburn. His gaze moved slowly around the camp.

Clinton was staring up at him. "Billy is dead," Clinton told him.

A muscle worked in Fisher's heavy-jowled face. His eye twitched. He glanced at the water, at the rising sun, back at Merrick. After a moment he sat down in front of his food.

Merrick carried a plate and a cup of coffee up the slight incline to the wagon. Butler was propped against the wheel.

Butler gave him a level smile, nodded his thanks. He drank the coffee and began to eat greedily.

Merrick glanced at Butler's bandages, found them only faintly blood-tinged.

161

He went to the rear of the wagon, took out two small army shovels. He tossed them down the incline so they fell near Clinton.

"You'll find my brother's grave down that incline, Clinton," he said, voice cold and meaningful. "You might dig your son's grave beside it."

# 13

CLINTON did not move for a
long time. Finally, he cleaned
the scraps from his plate, tossed it
along with the fork beside the smoldering
fire. He picked up the two shovels.

For a second he held one as if it were a
club. His red-rimmed eyes were fixed on
Merrick up the incline beside the wagon.
Merrick stood there, watching him.

"Come on, Perch," Clinton said.

The big gunman got up, tossing his
plate and cup beside Clinton's. He was
still groggy and massaged at his tousled
head where Merrick had hit him. He
took one of the shovels and the two
men walked between the wagon and
the boulder to the clearing where Billy
Clinton's body was twisted on the ground.

Valerie remained sitting on a stone
near the pool. She did not glance toward
Merrick or her husband. She turned

slightly so that she could watch Clinton and Perch Fisher digging out in the clearing. She stayed like that, her hands locked, immobile.

Merrick walked down the incline. He kicked sand into the fire and fanned away the last flare of smoke. He looked at Valerie a moment, but she did not turn. Clinton and Perch were working slowly, but turning deep spadefulls of earth each time. They spoke infrequently, and stopped to glance down the incline toward the sump where Merrick and their guns were.

It seemed to Merrick that the very look of the world this morning reflected his own inner disturbed feelings. The sun had given a coppery cast to the sky, to the few clouds that fringed the lower ceiling, and to the alkali ground. There was no breeze. It was already hot, though the sun was barely visible. It would be a hot and breathless day. He sighed, thinking it was going to be a deadly one.

He glanced toward Clinton and Perch. The earth was hard to dig in, and the work was slow. His mouth twisted. He knew that, for he had dug in that same ground. He tried to calculate how long it would take them to bury the boy.

He glanced toward the dull, coppery ball of sun. "We ought to be pulling out of here."

Valerie did not answer.

Jeff pulled higher against the wheel. "Mr. Merrick?"

For an instant, Valerie's head pulled around and she stared at her husband, face pallid. Then she exhaled, turned again to watch the men digging in the clearing.

Merrick went up the incline.

Butler said, "I'm feeling a lot better this morning."

"You feel up to traveling?"

"You mean would I rather take a chance on bleeding to death in a moving wagon than lying here waiting for those Apaches to come back. Help me up there and let's go."

"Then you have nothing against going south?"

A shadow flickered in Butler's eyes. "I've everything against it — but after all, you have my gun, mine host."

"Yes. I reckon that changes things all right."

"I've lain here, Merrick, heard old Clinton offer you a thousand dollars, heard Valerie plead with you, and Fisher threaten to kill you. Looks like nothing we can say will turn you back from San Carlos."

"I'm afraid not — I've been in towns where kids died of epidemic fever."

"It's a long, lonely way to San Carlos."

"Yes."

"Through Indian territory."

"So I've been told."

"We're much nearer a Fort Ambush patrol to the north . . ."

"Yes."

"You were a soldier, Merrick. Common sense ought to tell you when to retreat."

"I was a sergeant — never on the general's staff."

Jeff Butler's pale face flushed. Then he grinned, and for him it was easy. He seldom let his anger show through his charm, which was something he wore on the surface.

"Then why not take the advice of a man who was?" he said, smiling.

Merrick glanced toward the men digging. "I've a lot to do if we're going to clear out of here as soon as they bury the boy. If that's all you wanted — "

"But it isn't." Butler's face grew warm again, and Merrick saw something happening to his eyes.

Butler lowered his voice, the whine disappearing, a kind of difficulty with his breathing showing in each word. "I've one more offer to make you, Merrick — if you'll turn north."

"Why, don't you save your breath?"

"Won't you even listen? I think I can change your mind."

Merrick had turned away. Now he heeled around, his voice sharp. "All right. Let's have it."

"Let's talk it over a moment, Merrick."

A look of bitterness showed in Butler's handsome face. "I've seen the way you've looked at Valerie.

"What are you talking about?"

"Oh, let's not get upset. You see — I've seen the way she looks at you, too." His laugh had a rancid sound. "I've been sick, Merrick. Not blind."

"You're still sick."

Butler laughed at him. "You deny you want her?"

"I don't see the sense of talking about it at all."

"There's this sense . . . I know a real man when I meet up with one, Merrick. You're the first completely whole man I've met since the general I served with in Virginia. I admired that man, ungrudgingly . . . I can't say my admiration of you isn't a grudging kind. Because I can see without asking Valerie that she sees in you maybe the kind of man she thought I was when she married me. Though God knows, she should have known better even then."

"Is that all?"

Butler seemed not to have heard him. His mind was deeply entangled in his own, bitter memories, "She knows well enough now. I failed her back in the East, Merrick. I brought her out here with all kinds of glowing promises and I failed her worse than ever."

"That touches me. But there's nothing I can do about it."

Butler's mouth pulled into a hurting smile. "Yes. There is, Merrick. You can take advantage of it."

"I don't follow you."

"Yes, you do, Merrick. You're way ahead of me. You know and I know that after this Valerie is going to have an even lower estimation of me than before. If we get out of this alive, it'll be no thanks to me. Hell, I got us lost on a clear-marked trail and that got us into this hell in the first place."

"That happens."

"Yes. And it happens that when a woman finds herself married to a failure she can live with him — until she finds the kind of man she wants and —

deserves. You think I don't know the truth, Merrick? When we get out of this, if Valerie goes back East with me — if she stays with me at all — it will only be out of a sense of loyalty. It will be you she'll be thinking about."

"Maybe you can sleep this off."

"Take us to Tucson, Merrick. When we get there . . . I really got nothing to bargain any more. She despises me, she knows me for what I am — and worse, for what I'm not . . . Take us to Tucson — and I swear I'll step out of this, Merrick — Valerie will be free."

Merrick stared at Butler. The handsome man leaned against the wagon wheel, watching him, his dry eyes narrowed and tortured, near to tears that he would never shed. The breath was ragged across Butler's parted lips. He had sunk as low as a man could sink. He despised himself more than anyone else could. He had failed Valerie in every possible way and now that she was all he had left he was bartering her for his life — even as he was asking himself why he believed

170

anything as low as he was deserved to go on living.

The words struck Merrick hard, like the side of a hand across his Adam's apple. He swallowed hard, feeling blood surge against his temples. He was sure Butler could see the pulse bounce at the base of his throat.

His tongue touched his lips. They were parched. He moved his head to stare at the cool pool of water, suddenly thirsty. He let his gaze touch Valerie on the stone, the sun adding a coppery gloss to her red hair, the lines of her profile, the fullness of her breasts. He thought about her wild laughter and her stormy temper.

He inhaled deeply; his jaw tightened and he pulled his gaze away from her. He did not answer Butler.

Butler's bitter voice struck at him. "Deny you want her, Merrick? Last night, you thought I was asleep. I saw the way you looked at her. This morning when she might have killed you with my gun. She couldn't do it — "

"You make many deals like this for her?" Merrick was giving Butler a chance to flare into anger, to forget the suggestion he had made.

Jeff kept his voice low. "Look at her, Merrick. You know better than that. I've had — her loyalty. You could have — " Butler swallowed hard and did not finish that.

Merrick scowled. He wanted to walk away. He wanted to kick Butler's face. He did not move.

Butler's voice quavered. He was an ill man, a frightened one. "Listen to me, Merrick. You don't know what she's meant to me. But I know what she sees now when she looks at me — and it kills me. All I can save out of this hell is — maybe my life. I'm trying to buy my life. This is all I know. All I have."

Merrick stared at him.

"I know how scarce any woman is out here, Merrick . . . and you've never seen anything like Valerie — not anywhere."

"Then get her out of here."

"Can I do it? I'm doing what I can

for her. You better think about what you can do for yourself, Merrick. There are a lot of Apaches between here and San Carlos — between here and anywhere."

Merrick did not answer.

"You think you'll ever see a woman like Valerie again?"

"Does she know you're — offering to leave her like this?"

"What do you care? Stop being holy. What difference does it make?"

"None, I reckon." Merrick turned, drawing his tongue across his parched lips again.

Butler's voice grabbed after him. "Make up your mind, Merrick. Turn north — to Tucson."

Merrick strode away from the wagon going down the incline. It seemed to him the sun had climbed crazily, burning the earth, drying him out, dehydrating his body. His eyes throbbed with the blood pumped fast behind them. A lizard skittered between the rocks and he felt himself go taut. They'd pulled his nerves tight, stringing them thin in the sun to stretch and dry and break.

"Merrick."

Valerie's voice touched at him as he passed the stone where she sat. Her voice was troubled.

He paused, stopped, legs apart, staring at her. His eyes felt hot and the pressure against them made them ache. She was a coppery blur before him. He felt the muscles in his stomach tighten. He closed his fists, turned to walk away from her.

"Merrick."

He stopped but did not look at her.

"They — they're almost ready. Let's go, Merrick. Please . . ."

He did not answer. He could hear Clinton's lowered voice from the clearing, hear the clods of earth as they struck the sides of the open grave, filling it. He could feel Butler's strangely dry gaze on him from the wagon. The sun scorched his shoulders and the back of his neck.

He walked to the edge of the water. He glanced across his shoulder and over

Valerie's head to Clinton and Perch in the clearing.

He removed his gun belt, placed it on the ground close beside his boot. He pulled roughly at his shirt, jerking the buttons through the buttonholes, dragging his shirttails out of his belt.

He wore no undershirt. His back was baked brown, and muscles corded his shoulders, making lines to his lean hips. He dropped his shirt behind him, sank to his knees at the water's rim.

He cupped his hands and brought them brimming to his fevered face. This was not enough, and he bent forward, immersing his head in the cold water. He thought grimly, *This cold water can save a man more ways than one.*

He brought water up in his cupped hands, drinking thirstily, feeling the water falling against his chest, running along his flat stomach.

He bathed his eyes and then straightened up on his heels.

He could smell her. There was a warm, fresh excitement about her that was going to haunt him all the rest of his life. In that moment, crouching there, he could see his life, stretching hot and lonely ahead of him.

He had not heard her walk down close behind him, yet he knew he could turn and she would be there at his back.

"Blade."

There was something new in his name when she spoke it. She gave it a softness, she made a caress out of it. An old family name they'd given him in a burst of parental pride in bloodline. Funny what her voice could do to that name.

Merrick stood up slowly. The water ran down his face from his hair, off the squared planes of his jaw to his shoulders.

"Look at me, Blade."

And he thought, *The hell with everything else. The living, empty hell with loneliness, and what a man ought to do. What was a man to live with when he was alone? What he might have done, or what he had done? What else did a man regret except the good things he had left undone?*

There were a lot of Apaches between her — and anywhere.

Water coursed into the corners of his mouth. He felt his heart slugging against his ribs, knew that whatever had happened to Butler's eyes, happened now to his.

He turned around, suddenly, hands coming up from his sides.

He heard her catch her breath in a gasp that had horror in it. Her mouth sagged open, her green eyes distended, staring at the scar across his bare chest.

The life flowed downward out of him. He wanted to move, to speak, to curse; the anger and the agony was in him, but not the force.

His mouth twisted, and his eyes stung. Sure, a man lived with a scar, even one like this, for six years, it became part of him, and he lived with it, like any other infirmity. Sometimes, even, in moments like this one, a man forgot it entirely. God help him, after the look in her face, it would be a long time before he forgot it again.

His own gaze pulled down to the livid, jagged mark made by a knife, running from under his right collar bone like a streak of fantastic lightning across his rib cage, almost to his belt line. It had been laid bare by a knife, had healed this much, and would never heal any more.

His throat tightened. He stared down at her, hating the look of horror he saw in her pallid face. He wanted to rail at her. Not every man lived through hell and came out of it looking beautiful like Jeff Butler — if she wanted beautiful men, let her stay with her husband. But he didn't say any of that.

His voice grated, and he muttered between clenched teeth, "Next time you'll let a man know before you walk up on him like this."

The shock seeped out of her face, and something else replaced it. He did not see it. He didn't want to look at her any more.

He bent down, snatched up his shirt, thrust his arms into it.

She shook her head slowly, touched at her lips with her tongue. She tried to speak, but there was nothing to say, no words.

He picked up his gunbelt then, not even stopping to buckle it on. He strode away from her.

**M**ERRICK walked back to his rumpled blanket beside the boulder. Around him were the pans, the tin plates and cups, the ashes of the fire. Behind the small rock and under the boulder were the guns he'd stashed away. But he was not thinking about any of this.

He stood rigid for a moment, admitting the truth.

He was thinking about a saloon in Tucson. There was sawdust on the floor, and it was cool inside, out of the sun. The bartender knew him by name, but not by his capacity. Sometimes he went into the saloon and ordered a whiskey straight, and only one, never more. It would be something to see the bartender's face when he ordered a bottle and held his hand on its neck while he drank. The bartender would stare, thinking there was some mistake, thinking he didn't know Blade Merrick after all. Hell, who ever really knew any other person?

He buttoned his shirt, stuffing it into his trousers. Hell, a man had more than he could do on this earth even getting to know himself. Well, he had walked away from her. Not away from the soft flesh of her, the excitement of her hair, and the soft fragrance of her body. He had walked away from the look of horror in her face. He told himself he was glad he had done it, and the hell with the reason why. Only, all the time he knew what he wanted, and what he would always want.

He had to get things together, get that wagon out of here. The roast horsemeat would delay the Apaches for a while. It pleased him that they would gorge themselves first, but it was past time to hit the trail.

He buckled on his belt, his mind warning him it was time to leave, but his body longed to turn north, throw that goddam medicine out in the dirt. Maybe the Apaches would drink it, get drunk, even die from overdosage. He could turn north to Tucson, and that saloon. But the hell of it was, he was too honest. The saloon was only an excuse for thinking about Tucson. He wanted to get drunk; she was a poison in his bloodstream and he had to drink her out. But he knew if he went to Tucson he would have her. There weren't men enough; they didn't build walls high enough to keep him away from her.

He gathered up the cooking utensils, the plates and cups, dropping them into a sack. When he turned to go to the wagon he saw that Clinton and Perch were already there. They had thrown their shovels into the wagon bed. They were hunkered beside Butler and Valerie.

He stood there, watching them, knowing what they were saying without hearing the words. Clinton had some last-ditch plan. Clinton glanced toward Merrick, whispering urgently. Merrick saw Butler nod his head, and nod again. Butler's smile was charming, ingratiating.

He knelt down, gathered up the guns thonged together with a strip of leather. Carrying them under his right arm, dragging the sack, he went up the incline.

"Sorry to break up the meeting," he said. He moved his gaze from Perch to Clinton. Funny what depriving these men of their guns did to them. Where was Perch Fisher's contemptuous smile? "Perch, you and Clinton go over to the overhang. You got anything over there, get it ready to pull out of here."

He dropped the thonged guns under the front seat of the wagon.

"In case that looks inviting to you people," he said, "I better tell you, I'll shoot the first one of you that goes near that wagon until I give the word." He moved his gaze slowly across their faces, staring coldly at Valerie, including her. "You get the message?"

Clinton and Perch were on their feet. They did not answer, but walked slowly across the clearing to the overhang.

Merrick looked at Butler and Valerie for a moment. He turned on his heel, strode away.

He was almost to the clearing when Valerie's voice stopped him.

He paused and when she put out her hand asking him to stop, he leaned against a boulder where he could watch Clinton and Butler. A mouse skittered from a shattered rock across a sunny patch of ground to another shadow.

"I — want you to forgive me, Blade," she said.

"Nothing to forgive."

"Yes. I was startled when I saw that scar — "

"You're wasting time."

"No. I'm trying not to. There's something I must say. Jeff and I had talked all night — planning, not knowing what to do. Thinking — "

"About Tucson?" His voice was cold.

Her face colored faintly. Then her chin tilted.

"Everything just piled up, one shocking

thing after another — "

"It doesn't matter. I told you it doesn't matter."

"First, last night when you killed Billy. I — know. You had to. It was your life or his. But he was so young. Just a boy. The thought of his dying shocked and upset me. Please understand."

His voice was chilled. "I know only one thing. Boy or not, if I hadn't killed Billy Clinton, someone else would have."

She nodded, her head lowered.

He persisted, voice rough. "He'd followed his old man too far. Once he might have been worth saving. I don't know."

"It's that it all added up to upset me — "

"And there's one more thing." He was speaking more to himself now than to her. "Somebody killed my brother. Right here at this water hole — somebody like the Clintons."

"The Clintons?"

"Three men. Men who'd robbed a

Tucson bank and were on the run. All I know is they have saddlebags full of money — and now they're running north."

"But you have no proof."

"No. No proof."

She drew in a deep breath. She stared at his face, glanced over her shoulder at Butler sprawled beside the wagon, Clinton and Perch across the pool.

"I have something to tell you. I've got to tell you. No matter which way you plan to go."

He waited, watching her pallid face.

"They're going to jump you — they mean to take the wagon."

"I know that. You should be glad. The Clintons are going your way."

She bit her lip. "Maybe you knew they would jump you. But there's more. They talked it all over with Jeff and me."

"I didn't think you were exchanging recipes."

"Jeff told them he's willing to stand the trip — running all the way."

"Yes."

Her voice fell away. "They want me to — to let you — to get this gun from you — and remove the bullets."

His mouth was bitter. "I must be wearing what I want on my face. Everybody seems to know I've developed one weakness — and it's you."

"They hope so. They're gambling on it. They sent me after you now. They're watching — waiting."

He lifted his gaze from her face, feeling the working of the pulse in his throat. He wanted to laugh. Butler was staring at the sky, too casual. Clinton and Perch Fisher were talking together, watching something in another direction.

His mouth twisted. "Why the change of heart? Why are you telling me this?"

She shook her head. Her eyes filled with helpless tears. She looked away, staring at the clear pool with the boulders and the sky reflected in it.

She spread her hands. "I'm betraying my own husband."

"I asked you why."

Her voice went sharp. "I don't know

why. Yes — I do. I know what he wanted me to do — to get him safely to Tucson. I — would do it, but maybe I'd never feel the same again toward him. I don't know."

"Are you hitting back at him already?"

"No. I know what you have done for me. And for Jeff. I know what Clinton is, and Perch. No matter what they say, I'm afraid to trust them. And — even though you won't turn north, it's you I trust. Suddenly, it's only you. I seem to know that my very life depends on you."

She looked up at him, her eyes tear-brimmed. "And then — when I saw the look in your face — there by the pool, I knew something I'd not known before. I knew you were a good man. Maybe the last good man I'll ever know. I could betray Jeff . . . but I couldn't betray you — not any more."

She pressed her knotted fist against her mouth. Tears struck her knuckles.

"All right." He kept his voice low. "Go back to them. Stall. Tell them you will come back to me — and that I want you to. That ought to please them."

She nodded, turned and walked slowly away from him.

He stepped away from the boulder, looking at her. He felt an emptiness he'd never known.

He raised his voice. "Clinton. Perch. Move over to the wagon. I'll get up on the knoll and take a last look around. But stay away from those guns. I can see you just as easy from up there as I can from here."

He climbed the knoll, feeling the sun on his back. He glanced back at the four people beside the wagon. Valerie was talking dully to them. They watched him, but did not move toward the guns under the seat. Those guns were tied together. It would take time to loose one of them, and it might not be loaded. Merrick could kill any of them from the knoll. Common sense told them to trust Valerie's body and its magnetism for him, and to wait . . .

He scanned the land before him, an inescapable feeling of wrong building in him. It was the sense of being trapped that he'd first felt when Billy Clinton shot the Apache scout yesterday afternoon, mixed now with all that had happened within the confines of the water wells, and all the unknown things that were happening with the Apaches out there somewhere in the wilderness.

He fixed his gaze on the far reaches of the heatswept land. Beyond, the crumpled badlands mountains lay against the sky, looking purple and cool. He pulled his gaze back to the flat, empty land between. The sun sucked the last moisture remaining from the night out of every plant, every grain of sand. A dust-devil rolled lazily, a hawk poised high in the stark, faded blue of the sky.

There was no movement out there, no trace of the Apaches. It didn't make sense that they had abandoned the hunt for the people they'd attacked in the valley, or that they would forgive the murder of the scout.

There was no sign of them in the vast tableland. The sun was coppery on the earth. A thought struck him. The Apaches may have moved up here last night. It would have been easy following the wheel tracks he'd left for them yesterday.

He leaned against the boulder, thinking about this. They had feasted on roast horse, followed a clear trail. He was almost afraid to turn and look behind him.

The first time he heard the sound beyond the forest of piñon and mesquite he tried to tell himself it was thunder, the pound of hooves, the beat of his own heart. But he knew better. It was the slow measured beat of a drum.

He stood there only a moment after that sound was repeated. He knew it was a good way to lose his scalp, but the desire to know outweighed his fear. He drew his gun, ran across the rocky ground and went as silently through the mesquite as he could move to the place where they had buried the Apache.

He stood there staring at the mesquite bush thrown aside, the grave open, and the Apache's body gone. He decided this was the moment when a man's whole life flashed through his mind. No matter what he had hoped for before, it was all over now. All wiped out by the mournful throb of the Apache drum out there below him.

Sweat coursed down his face. For a moment he could not pull himself away from that grave.

Hell, he thought, now I can't even go south.

He turned and walked blindly back to the clearing. He carried his gun at his side, but hardly knew he was carrying it.

He reached the rim of the descent to the water hole. He glanced over his shoulder. Nothing had changed; yet nothing was ever going to be the same again. The sun beat against the rocks, sucked life from the earth, glittered in the dust, but worse than the sun was the drum. It was everywhere, throbbing slowly like the last measured beats of a man's heart.

He walked slowly down the incline. Trying to think, but unable to do anything with the drum throbbing in the pit of his stomach, he moved toward the wagon.

He saw they were watching him. They had heard the drum, and knew what it meant, and suddenly he was their last hope. He wanted to laugh, looking at them. Butler had become the shade of ashes after a rain, and was chewing at his lips. Valerie stood immobile against the wagon. In her eyes were some of the swirling terrors he had seen there after the attack in the valley yesterday. All of it brought back to her by the pound of the drums. Perch, standing beside the blanket, reached instinctively for the gun that was no longer at his hip.

Charley Clinton stood staring up the incline toward the piñon forest and the sound of the drums. His legs were apart; sweat streaked his dust-patted face.

"Drums," Clinton said to Merrick. "The Indians out there?"

Merrick nodded. His mouth pulled into a bitter grin and his gaze struck hard against Clinton's. "You can quit worrying about the wagon — and which way you're going, Charley."

"We got any chance to get out of here?"

"None that I know. Not and get away from them. They found the Apache we buried and they dug him up. They're giving him an Apache burial. I figure we got until they get him cleansed of white burial and safely consigned to their gods."

"Hell," Perch Fisher said. "How much time we need? Let's get out of here."

# 15

"I GOT no hope they'll let us out of here," Merrick said, "but there's just one way to find out."

He nodded toward Butler, and Clinton moved with him to the wounded man on the blanket. They knelt on each side of him.

"How do you feel, Butler?" Merrick said.

"I'm too scared to feel anything," Butler said. "Let's go."

Merrick smiled at him, liking him for the first time since he'd known him. You had to admire anyone man enough to admit out loud to fear.

"Careful," Merrick said to Clinton. "Move him slow. We don't want to start him bleeding."

"Just move," Butler said, shaking his head. "My blood isn't going to run as numb as I am."

They lifted the wounded man. Valerie shook out the blanket and placed it in the body of the wagon. They set Butler inside the wagon.

Perch gathered up the three saddle bags and dropped them into the wagon.

Merrick laughed at him, but Perch said, "There's a lot of money there, Merrick, and as long as there's a chance I'll live to spend it, I'm hanging on to it."

Merrick shrugged. He told Valerie to get into the wagon. He helped her under the canvas with her husband.

"All right, Perch," he said. "You ride back there with the girl and the money."

Clinton spoke levelly. "There's one little matter, Merrick."

Merrick heeled around. "Yes?"

"We best throw in together until we get out of this here little difficulty, Merrick," Clinton said. "I hope you see fit to give us back our guns — or do you intend to let us bite our way past them Apaches?"

Merrick grinned and swung up on the front of the wagon. He loosed the thongs, tossed down rifles and pistols to Perch and Clinton.

"I admire you, Clinton," he said. "Admire the way you can make deals."

Clinton's mouth pulled into a wolfish grin. He stood a moment listening to the pound of the drums out there and the sudden wail of frenzied Indians.

"I'll make any deal, Merrick, that will get me what I want." He jerked his head toward the rear of the wagon. "Perch and me got that money — and we ain't dead yet."

Clinton climbed up on the seat. Merrick told him to pull the wagon around and head out of the sump, moving slowly.

Merrick ran across to the boulder where he'd built a fire. He kicked out all traces of the fire, pushed the discolored and fire-blackened stones into the pool.

He cut a scraggly mesquite brush and followed the wagon up the incline, brushing away all the wagon tracks and hoof marks. He had an empty feeling of futility about all this, but, like Clinton, he'd do what he had to, and he wasn't dead yet.

"Let's go," Perch whispered from the rear of the wagon. Clinton had stopped at the rim of the knoll.

Merrick glanced over his shoulder. That water hole looked peaceful, quiet, belonging to eternity.

He swung up on the seat beside Clinton. "Keep those horses light. One horseshoe against one rock and we'll interrupt that burial."

Clinton slapped the reins softly, the horses strained, and the wagon rolled out on the rocks.

From beyond the wooded area came the chanting cries of the reburial ceremony, and the sudden, rasping screams of hatred.

Clinton shuddered. "Sounds like that, makes a man think on his sins, all right."

Merrick sat tensely, rifle across his knees, a finger against its trigger. He watched all the land ahead of them, but it was tricky, a dangerous place of boulders, of brush, seeming open and flat, but now full of concealment for watching Apaches.

Clinton's voice was low. "Merrick, I been thinking. Back there in the valley when we were attacked. It was a small raiding party. Not more than seven."

"Yeah?"

"So now Billy took care of one of them. That leaves six. They're over there in a ceremony. If we rushed in there right now, we could kill off them six before they got through wailing."

"You couldn't sell me that with a free gift on the side."

"Hell, man. They're in a frenzy of weeping — six of them."

"Six is plenty. There never were too many Apaches out here, but, mister, they'll remember the Apache as a warrior when all the other tribes are forgotten. You be glad the Army has 'em outnumbered in this territory, Clinton, or you'd be robbing banks east of the Mississippi right now."

Butler's voice came through the canvas. "What's there to see out there?"

"Nothing," Clinton told him. "You got a lot better view in there, mister. Enjoy it."

The wailing, keening cries of the Indians rose like dust into the sun, clouding and filtering out across the wasteland.

The wagon had rolled a few yards downslope with Clinton holding back on the reins. He glanced at Merrick. "You think it's about time to let 'em out, Mr. Merrick?"

"Ain't going to get any better," Merrick said. "Let's hit the road."

Clinton raised the reins high ready to slab them across the horses' rumps.

A rifle cracked almost at the animals' heads. The bullet whistled past like a hornet.

In that brief instant Merrick and Clinton considered the angles, the chances of running and getting out alive, the odds in favor of fighting back. Perch was concealed in the back, one more gun. But the army horses were too slow, they were hopelessly outnumbered, too far from any chance of aid.

"Hold it, Clinton," Merrick said. "Hold it hard. That shot meant stop. Next one is sure to mean one of us dead. If we got a chance at all of getting out alive — it'll be if we can talk our way out."

Clinton pulled hard on the reins.

The horses' heads came up high. Before they were quieted, three Indians stepped from behind boulders not nearly large enough to conceal them, yet they'd been concealed.

The three men held their rifles ready in the bend of their arms. Their faces were painted, and their bare chests were streaked with symbols. Their black hair was tied tightly against their heads.

Perch spoke from inside the wagon. "What's wrong, Hardhead? What you stopping for?"

Hardhead Charley spoke from the side of his mouth. "Hold what you got, Perch. Don't none of you make some fool move that might get us killed."

Perch's voice was awed. "Apaches?"

"Shore don't resemble a delegation of Quakers."

There was silence from the body of the wagon.

"They know about the woman," Hardhead said from the corner of his mouth.

Merrick was staring at the Apaches. He had never seen any of the three before. They were young braves, would not have been on the trail six years ago, and had not been in any spots where they'd have met him since then.

"They know all about us," he said, wanting to silence Hardhead. "Keep your face straight no matter what they do."

One of the braves stepped forward beside the head of the right horse. He made a motion toward the rifle, the guns in their holsters. He jerked his head toward the ground.

"Throw 'em out," Merrick said, keeping his gaze level upon the braves. "Don't die a hero."

Clinton pulled his gun from its holster

with his fingertips, tossed it to the ground. He watched the Apaches but they did not smile at his comedy. He did not feel particularly like smiling, either.

Merrick lifted the rifle with both hands and tossed it outward at the feet of the Apaches. The Apaches barely looked at it, stood waiting for the handgun.

Merrick drew it from his holster, spun it and caught it by the barrel so they would not misread his intentions. He listened, heard the continued wailing from the burial. This was a tune of evil for them — white men had desecrated one of their party, buried him flat in white-man fashion, a white man's burial for an Apache brave. It would take much wailing, much frenzy to cleanse this one's soul for eternity; it would take much blood to wash away the indignity and the insult.

He tossed out the gun to the Apache. The coppery-fleshed man caught the gun, inspected it, pushed it into the top of his breechcloth.

They did not even glance toward the

rear of the wagon, though Merrick was certain they knew the two men and the woman were there. They were not concerned with what they could not see at the moment. They were very cold.

The brave now made a motion that told them to turn the wagon back toward the Wells.

Clinton nodded and pulled the heads of the horses around. Horseshoes clopped against outcroppings of stone. Merrick knew this was no longer important.

He heard the stifled crying of the woman inside the wagon. Something twisted inside him, but it did not displace the sense of helplessness that coursed through his body in his very bloodstream.

The measured pound of the drum struck against him, attacking his nerves at last.

The three braves walked silently beside the slow-moving wagon.

Clinton exhaled. "Dammit to goodbilly hell, Merrick. I told you yesterday afternoon. We ought to run. Yesterday. Before that scout showed."

"Run?" Merrick's voice was sharp and low. "Run where, Clinton? North? Right to them?"

"Hell, we had a chance yesterday, Merrick. What kind of chance we got now?"

"The same one we had yesterday."

"No. Yesterday them Apaches would have had full bellies and a roast-horse hangover. They wouldn't have had this here killing they had to avenge. Way they felt yesterday they might have wanted to get back to their squaws."

"You believe that?"

"Maybe not. But we were better off yesterday than we are today."

The wagon rolled slowly, with the gait of a hearse, Merrick thought, up the incline and then started down toward the water hole.

It was the same water hole, but that was all. Everything about it was changed.

The drum had stopped from above the sump. Now there was silence. The three Apaches had moved through the mesquite and walked down the incline, leading the ponies.

The brave beside the wagon held up his hand. Clinton closed his fists on the reins. The horses stood poised. The three Apaches at the well did not turn around. They led the ponies to the water, allowed them to drink.

While the ponies drank, the brave who had ordered the guns thrown down went to the rear of the wagon. He threw back the flaps.

Merrick sat motionless on the boot. He heard Perch and Valerie get out of the wagon. The brave spoke then, his voice sharp.

Merrick knew he was telling Butler to get out of the wagon.

Perch said, "He's wounded. We'll have to help him out."

The Apache understood Perch Fisher. He said, voice cold, "Out."

Merrick did not move. He heard Butler crawl to the tail gate, try to pull himself over. He heard his frantic grasping and then heard the thud as his body struck the earth. The two braves nearest the wagon stared at him with interest but the three at the water seemed to hear none of this.

Valerie cried out.

"Up," the brave ordered.

Merrick stared straight ahead. He felt the wagon vibrate as Butler reached up and pulled himself to his feet against it.

The brave marched them forward around the wagon. Merrick saw then that he had the rest of their rifles. This seemed a very unimportant matter.

Butler staggered. Valerie caught his arm trying to support him, but he shook her hands down. He swayed slightly, but stood there tall, biting down on his mouth, sweat coursing down his forehead from his rumpled, curly hair. The side of his handsome face was dirt-smeared where he'd fallen onto the ground from the wagon. *By God,* Merrick thought with pride, *the devil was on the general's staff.*

The brave jerked his head at Clinton and Merrick. Merrick glanced at Hardhead. He nodded toward the ground. "After you."

Clinton swung down, stood with legs apart, returning the cold stares of the Indians.

Merrick sprang from the wagon, stood beside Charley. The three braves walked behind them, prodded them forward on the incline.

One of the warriors at the pool led the last of the ponies away. Only then did the other two turn and inspect their prisoners, eyes chilled and contemptuous.

The taller stepped forward. No one had to introduce him as the leader. He may have been a minor chief of one of the roving tribes. Merrick did not know. He had never seen him before. But you didn't have to be acquainted to see the royal lineage he was heir to.

He was bare to the waist, as were the others. His face was marked along each cheek with a single yellow line. He held his corded shoulders straight, and his head was erect. His cheeks were hollowed, high-planed; he was a man who lived often with hunger, but when his belly was empty he had his pride.

All of this was in his face, in the way he stood, and in the very way he studied the white people before him.

He let his gaze move over them, pulled his eyes back around, faced Merrick. "You are the leader of these people?" His voice was hesitant; the white man's language was a hateful thing as well as difficult.

Merrick lifted his shoulders, let them drop. "I will speak for them."

The leader's cold smile said there would not be a great deal to say. He jerked his head toward the wagon. "Crosses?"

"The army," Merrick said. "They thought they might mean something. I didn't. I was carrying medicines."

"Only medicines?" The Apache looked at the woman and the other three men.

"I picked up what you left, yesterday," Merrick said.

"And killed a brother of mine."

"About this I am sorry."

The Indian's face went rigid. He said, "If you do a thing, keep your pride in it

209

when you die for it. It will not keep you alive to whine and beg."

"I neither whine nor beg. Still, I regret that death."

"And I spit out your apologies. I would admire more a man who could die proud of what he has done. And for that death you will die. You already died when you pulled the trigger that killed my brother."

Valerie caught her breath in a sob. Merrick spoke quickly, trying to pull the Apache's attention from her cry.

"You will see me die without asking mercy of you," Merrick said.

"The coyote brays loud before the trap springs on his throat. We shall see how you die. Believe that." He stepped back, dragging his cold gaze across them. "Vittorio has spoken."

# 16

THERE was a moment of intense, bitter silence. The Apache chieftain stood with his arms at his sides. One might have thought him relaxed except that his fists were tightly clenched, the muscles twisted in hard cords up his arm. The sun burned down upon the back of Merrick's neck. He watched the dust settle across the Wells, heard the patient slobbering of the ponies, the switch of their tails; but there was no end to the silence.

He heard Clinton's intake of breath when the Apache named himself for them. Merrick did not look but knew that Perch Fisher had sagged slightly, the hope dying in him. Neither man now felt so certain there was some way out, a time left for them to spend the loot in those swollen saddlebags. They had roamed the wastelands without meeting

Vittorio face to face until today. They had heard of him.

The brave who had ordered them from the wagon was standing close behind Valerie. Merrick saw Vittorio's gaze pull from them to Valerie and he turned his head slightly enough to see what had attracted Vittorio's attention.

The brave was holding Valerie's red hair in his hands, letting it flow through his fingers. Then he drew the back of his hand softly across her cheek and down along her throat. He saw that Valerie shivered, that her eyes had the wild look of terror in them, but she stood perfectly still. In the sagged pull of her mouth he saw that she had abandoned hope, too. She did not know Vittorio's name or his reputation, but she was a woman and she could read his hatred and contempt in his face. There was not an atom of mercy in his black eyes.

The brave could not keep his hands off her.

In the Mescalero tongue, Vittorio snapped at the brave to cease.

The other braves stared at the young warrior and at Valerie. They laughed, but it was a brief sound, quickly dead and lost in the heat and stillness.

The brave reluctantly pulled his hands away from her, then caressed her cheek one more time with the backs of his fingers. He let his gaze move over her and then he walked forward to Vittorio.

The young brave, as tall as Vittorio, heavier, still lacked the arrogant look of strength the leader had. He had never known the hunger and the suffering Vittorio had known, and this deprived him of inner strengths rather than increasing them.

He spoke haltingly, in supplication and with much humility. At the same time there was urgency in the request he made. Merrick heard the brave ask for the woman. He was making promises of exchanges and sacrifices.

Clinton said, "The brave is asking for Butler's wife."

Merrick said, "Yes."

He heard Valerie's sobbing intake of breath.

Clinton said, "He wants the woman left alive — when the rest of us are killed."

Again Valerie caught her breath. Merrick glanced at her, afraid she would fall. His anger rose sharply at Clinton, then subsided.

"All right," he said. "Drop it."

"What the goodbilly hell," Clinton said. "She might as well know what's going to happen to her."

"We all know what's going to happen to us," Merrick said, speaking between clenched teeth. "You worry about how you'll take it when your turn comes."

Clinton laughed at him. The very existence of this final moment of danger gave the old pirate a sense of courage that would see him into eternity. Merrick could not help admiring the old man who had lived out his evil existence, taking what he wanted and asking nothing of anyone.

He touched his gaze upon the beefy

Fisher and found him gone to lard. He was sweating, the streaks showing along his face and thick neck and upon his shirt. Merrick did not condemn Fisher for his fear. Fisher, like every other man who ever sat around a campfire out here at night, had heard tales of Indian tortures — and the Apache knew all the vulnerable areas of a man's body. They could keep you alive long after you wished you were dead.

Clinton watched the brave begging Vittorio for the right to keep the woman as his prize of this raid.

He turned slightly, glancing at Butler. His scraggly beard pulled beside his mouth. "Well, Butler, here's another chance for you. Maybe you can stay alive by trading off your woman to them Injuns."

Tears welled in Butler's eyes. He tried to stand straighter, but was too weak. He swayed slightly. A muscle worked in his jaw, but he did not answer Clinton. He did not look at him, but stared straight ahead of him.

Merrick looked at Valerie, saw that in a moment she was going to faint.

Vittorio lifted his hand and the brave stepped back. Obviously, though Vittorio had promised nothing, the brave was hopeful. There was a touch of excitement about his face and he was staring at Valerie.

Merrick met Vittorio's gaze. He kept his face rigid, and did not lower his eyes under the chieftain's stare. The Apache chief was not impressed. He would yet see how arrogant the white man remained.

Merrick said, "So you are Vittorio?"

"You have heard of me?"

"I have heard of you. But I have never heard that you killed a wounded man." He nodded toward Butler whose stark white face showed the agony he endured standing there. But Butler remained erect, eyes forward. The old Confederate general would have been proud of his staff officer, Merrick thought.

He said, "Vittorio the brave kills wounded men and gives the man's wife as a prize. Too bad I will not live after today. I would have a new story to tell about Vittorio the brave.

A slow flush crawled upward under Vittorio's flesh. He stepped toward Merrick.

Merrick did not flinch, kept his voice level and low, and deadly. "We are travelers, crossing your land in peace. We are not soldiers. The army wagon you see there is loaded with medicine. Is the Apache no longer a man that he must rob women and prey on the helpless?"

For an agonizing moment stretched long in time, Vittorio stared at Merrick. It looked as though Merrick had taunted the Apache beyond endurance and the man would kill him with his bare hands. That was what Vittorio wanted to do. There was no one at the water hole who could doubt that. Vittorio's fingers opened, closed, made an involuntary gesture toward Merrick's throat. He had moved the remaining distance between them, hardly seemed aware he had strode forward. He breathed through his mouth and in those dark eyes the hatred smoldered, while Vittorio remembered he was a prince and this was a white man, not worthy of forcing him to lose control for even a second.

Vittorio took one step back. The anger had subsided and he was master again. He swept his gaze across his captives, looking at Valerie as though she, being a woman, did not exist.

He spoke to the brave who wanted her as his prize. The brave nodded, ran to the rear of the wagon. He inspected the boxes there, brought one and placed it at Vittorio's feet. They watched as Vittorio jerked his head and the brave ripped open the box. Vittorio stared at the bottles of medicine.

"Medicine," Clinton said. "All medicine. A town dies of fever and we head there." He nodded toward the south.

Vittorio did not look at Clinton. The Apache despised a liar and Vittorio did not bother to remind the big man that he had left them yesterday with a burning wagon that was headed north.

Vittorio spoke to the braves around them. The Apaches sprang to obey him. Working in pairs, the Apaches caught the white men, two at the arms, two at the feet, and slung them to the ground almost as if they were sheep to be sheared. They tied their wrists, staked them out, arms and legs spread wide.

It was accomplished speedily. Perch was the only one who fought. The butt of a rifle driven into his face took the fight out of him. Staked out on the ground, Perch rolled his head back and forth.

Merrick stared up at Valerie. The buck who desired her was standing at her back. He held her wrist, her arm twisted between her shoulder blades. This brave had lost some of the excitement of the torture in anticipation of carrying the woman to his lodge.

Merrick rolled his head, saw that Butler had been staked out beside him. Butler was in agony — they had broken open his wound. His bandage was stained the brownish-red of blood. Butler could not bite back the whimpering sounds of pain burned out of him by the bleeding wound in his side.

Merrick kept his voice low, hoping that Vittorio standing above them would not hear his words. "Try to swallow it, boy. There's no quicker way to get fed to the dogs — Apaches hate tears."

Vittorio strode tall and erect along the row of staked-out captives. His smile was full of contempt.

He looked over each of them slowly, particularly caught by the sight of Butler's blood darkening the bandage about his belly.

Vittorio said, "There is a question I will ask of you white men. It will buy you nothing to answer it, and yet for the one who answers it, I might order the torture ceased. This I do not promise. First I must hear your answer."

Perch rolled his head back and forth. His nose was bleeding. The other men remained still. The sun blazed into their faces, stinging the tears into their eyeballs.

"My question," Vittorio said. "I want one of you to name the man who shot my blood relative.

He waited. The silence pressed down upon them, and the sun blazed in their eyes. They did not move.

"You are very brave for now," Vittorio said. "I think maybe all of you will be begging to answer — soon." His mouth pulled and his gaze struck hard against Merrick's.

Vittorio paced before them. "I have so little regard for you — for all of you — that my blood is not appeased at the thought of watching you die crying and screaming in return for the death of my blood relative. That is not enough." His eyes distended and his mouth pulled back from his teeth. "I will give you something to live for. In a moment you will begin to die, one of you at the time. Each will have the pleasure of seeing the other die. If there is among you one who can endure Apache torture without tears — " he stared at Merrick who had insulted him — "prove yourself as much a man as any Apache is, I will allow all of you to live and go in peace from this place."

The buck holding Valerie cried out in protest. Vittorio raised his head slowly, and regarded the brave with a cold expression. For a moment protests bubbled across the buck's lips, but under the unrelenting stare of Vittorio they fell away.

Vittorio looked over the four men one more time. He walked back to the rim of the pool, stood with his back to them.

Merrick watched an Apache building a fire near them. There was a cry from another brave and Vittorio spun around on his heel.

The brave ran down the incline carrying the saddle bags. One was burst open and money spilled from it.

He dropped the saddlebags at Vittorio's feet. Vittorio said something to him, and he slashed open the other two bags, gold and Federal paper money spilling out.

Vittorio stared at the white men. His eyes were sardonic. "Medicine?"

"We are very rich men," Clinton said. "Why don't you take the money, buy yourself many rifles and let us go?"

"The money I will take," Vittorio said. He knelt, caught some of it in his fist. "Vittorio will spend it as he believes best. Let you go? You will buy your freedom, white man, in one way."

"Well, you tried," Merrick said to Clinton.

"As long as I'm alive, I will try, mister."

"Is that money from the bank at San Carlos?" Merrick said.

"I am pleased to tell you that it is," Clinton said. "We were headed north to spend it."

Merrick's mouth pulled taut. They were running north from San Carlos, just as a month ago the three of them had fled south from a bank robbery in Tucson. There was no longer any doubt why these men would have killed him rather than return with the army wagon south to San

Carlos. His instinct and his hatred had pointed straight and true at these men. They had ridden into the water hole, found Ab there, shot him in the back and left him to the ants. Killed him simply to leave no witnesses to their trail.

He closed his eyes against the burn of the sun but could not escape seeing in his mind the way his brother had died, imagining the pleasure his death had brought to these men. Suddenly he regretted dying at the hand of the Apaches. He had covered many days and many miles looking for these men and proof against them. Now when he had found them, it was too late.

He heard Butler scream, crying out. He jerked his eyes open. One of the braves was ripping away Butler's bandage. The blood spurted from the tear in his side, coursing along his bare stomach and staining his trousers. The Indians had cut away Butler's shirt. The wounded man was biting at his mouth until his lips bled, but it was no good. He could no longer swallow his agony.

# 17

VITTORIO jabbed his thumb toward the sobbing Butler. "This one," he said, speaking at Merrick and spitting out the words, "weak as a woman. Weaker."

"Let Vittorio speak sometime with a bullet in his belly and his blood lost for two days," Merrick said.

Vittorio laughed at him, a bitter sound. With his lance he pressed at the tear in Butler's side, toying with him almost without interest.

"We settle this one first," Vittorio said, "lest he escape us by dying before we can kill him."

"In the name of God," Butler pleaded. "I can't stand any more. I'm dying. Mercy. In the name of God. Mercy."

Vittorio stared at him without changing expression, applying slight pressure to the lance.

"I'll tell you who killed your brother," Butler wailed.

Vittorio shrugged. His face said that he had been sure Butler would speak.

"It was none of us," Butler wept. "I swear it. It was one who lies dead now. It was Billy Clinton." He jerked his head toward Hardhead Charley. "Ask him. It was his son — and his son is dead."

Hardhead's voice had ironic laughter in it, and not a trace of fear. "It was my son, Vittorio. My son Billy. He shot your brother. Yesterday."

Vittorio stared at Butler, then at Clinton. He waved his hand downward at Butler, drew the blood-tipped lance away. He stepped back.

Vittorio looked down at Butler. "My thanks to you. I leave your eyes to the buzzards."

He turned his back on Butler.

From where he was staked out, Merrick could see they were heating the barrel end of his rifle in the fire that blazed, paled against the coppery brilliance of the sun. The brave was not hurried; he turned the barrel slowly in the hottest part of the fire.

Vittorio walked along the line of staked men. His warriors walked with him, converging on Perch Fisher.

Vittorio spoke to one of them. The brave hunkered on his haunches beside Perch's head.

From the surface crust of the earth, the brave carefully scooped fine thin sand. At a signal from Vittorio, he caught Perch by the hair and jerked his head back.

Perch did not make a sound. The blood had coagulated along his cheeks so he looked almost as painted as the Apaches. The Indian twisted his fist in Perch's hair so he was forced to twist his head back as far as his neck would allow.

With his head held back in the iron grip of the Apache, Fisher's flesh was stretched taut.

The Apache held his head above Perch's face and funneled a slow, steady stream of sand into his nostrils. With interest the Apaches stood watching to see how long Perch could endure the torment. Perch opened his mouth, gasping air through it, but the sand filled his nose, spilled in his throat and suddenly he could no longer breathe at all.

Perch screamed, rolling his head back and forth, gasping, unable to speak.

Vittorio slashed his hand downward. The brave released Perch's head, stepped back from him. Vittorio stared at Perch for a moment, then spat on him.

Vittorio walked to Merrick, stared at him and then signaled toward Clinton. He strode forward, stood at Hardhead Charley's feet.

Clinton rolled his head on the side, staring at Merrick. "If you're impatient, Merrick, you can have my place in line."

Merrick lay there, staring at the sky as long as he could.

From the thicket the braves brought greasewood, carefully shaved off the thorns.

Merrick saw them place thorns under

each of Clinton's nails. The big man kept his face straight, his gaze fixed on the apex of the sky. With the flat of a knife they tapped the thorns into the quick under Clinton's nails.

His head rolled back and forth. He would lunge upward against his thongs but his face did not change, he did not speak.

When his nails were torn loose and his fingers were bloodied, Vittorio jerked his head at the braves. They jerked the thorns from Clinton's bleeding hands.

Vittorio gave another signal. Two braves loosed the thongs on Clinton's left side, and crossed over, yanking him over.

A brave came down the incline with a thick limb. Vittorio tested it against his palm, handed it back to the brave and nodded.

When they brought the limb down across Clinton's kidneys the breath was forced in a rush across his mouth. He did not cry out. He writhed each time the limb was brought down. They could not make him beg for mercy even after he began to spit blood.

Vittorio spoke. The braves yanked the rawhide, pulling Clinton over on his back again. The stakes were driven into the ground. Two braves ripped away Clinton's shirt.

The old man's face was pale. Blood bubbled from the corner of his mouth, trickled into his beard. His eyes were open but were glazed slightly, very dry.

Vittorio bent at the waist, staring at Clinton. "Why don't you weep, white man? Cry out and beg. This Vittorio would like to see."

Clinton did not move.

Vittorio gave a dry laugh, jerked his head at the brave heating the rifle mouth in the fire.

The barrel was white hot. The brave crossed to Clinton. Vittorio showed the gun to Clinton, nodded again.

Slowly the burning barrel was lowered toward Clinton's exposed navel. It touched his flesh. There was the acrid odor of burning flesh. Clinton moaned first, rolling his head back and forth, then he screamed, and kept screaming, the tears and the agony boiling from his mouth.

Vittorio sent the brave back to the fire. He stood at Merrick's feet until he decided the gun barrel was reheated properly. He spoke and the brave came running with the gun.

This time Vittorio himself handled the gun. He stepped forward standing across Merrick's chest. His mouth pulled into a taunting smile, the Apache stared down into Merrick's face.

Holding the gun by its butt, Vittorio lowered it straight down toward Merrick's eyes, moving slowly with deadly steadiness.

When the gun was still more than a foot away, Merrick felt the heat like lances ripping into his eyeballs. The white-hot gun barrel came closer. This was like having your eyes broiled in hell, like staring into the white hot ball of the midday sun, like having your soul burned from your body by fire.

The gun was so near now that he could not see it. He writhed against the thongs. He had been sure Vittorio would press the gun against his face, burning out his eyes, but, for the moment anyhow, the Indian stayed the rifle inches from his brow.

Merrick felt his eyes go dry, felt them burn, seeming to constrict and lose all their fluid in the heat. It was as it the heat were a magnet painfully drawing the color from the pupils. The pain lanced through his head, striking at the raw nerve ends at the base of his skull. He could hear himself yelling, screaming, begging for mercy, and yet there could not have been a sound from him because the gun was not drawn away.

He tried to roll away from the killing heat but slowly, patiently and relentlessly the gun followed his head as it rolled back and forth against the ground.

His teeth chattered. Please God, let them put out my eyes. Let it end. It can only end when I'm blind, God, let it end.

He felt the reason swirling and disappearing from his brain, drawn out of him by the white-hot magnet. Sudden crazy memories raced disjointed through his mind. The first pony he'd ever owned, given to him by his father on a farm in Virginia. The way Ab's body had looked pumped full of bullets and left beside the pool. The look in Valerie Butler's face when he had turned to her, scarred chest bared, from that pool. He could hear Mary Beth's screams, and she was no longer screaming for him to help her when he was helpless to aid her, she was begging them to kill her. They had not left her anything to live for, and by the time he had insanely chewed the thongs from his wrist and rushed at the men crouched over her, she was begging to die. He would not scream aloud. He would not ask any mercy of these people who had shown no mercy to his wife, making her live, making her suffer after she pleaded with them to let her die. He no longer knew if he were screaming, only that his head rolled on the earth and his eyes burned and there was no end to the burning.

He did not know how long Vittorio stood there, tracing his agonized rolls with the gun barrel. His wrists fought the thongs and half a dozen times they caught his arms and drove the stakes into the earth again.

The world had become a blazing inferno, a blanket of flowing blood even when he distended his eyes.

"Have mercy!" He heard a woman scream that. For an instant his brain told him it was Mary Beth, but Mary Beth was six years dead. It was Valerie who had cried out.

Suddenly the gun was gone from his face. He did not know now long it was gone. Even after the heated metal had been withdrawn, the agony burned into his eyes.

He stopped rolling his head. He stared into the sun, but saw nothing. There was a blur before his eyes.

Vittorio spoke, a sharp guttural order.

Vittorio had moved away, was standing at his feet.

Through the pain that blazed inside his head, he felt them tearing away his shirt. He stretched his head upward. Now they would press the reheated gun against his navel. Clinton had screamed and begged for mercy. In a moment the gun would touch his vital and tender area and he would scream too. He looked forward to it. The hell would end for a moment. There would be nothing left except for the Apaches to kill them then.

The shirt was ripped away. Blade lay there, waiting. There was a moment of terrible, stunned silence.

The blur did not lessen. It was as though he could see blood flowing across his eyeballs, and that was all he could see.

"Get back." He heard Vittorio yell that. It was spoken in the Apache dialect and the warriors fell away from the men staked on the ground.

Through the agony in Merrick's brain

came the realization that when they had ripped away his shirt Vittorio had been staring down at the knife scar across his chest.

Suddenly Vittorio lunged forward. Crouched over Merrick, he caught his throat in his right hand.

"Speak." The words spat through Vittorio's lips. "Your name, man."

"Merrick." Blade tried to hold his breath, to keep any quaver from his voice.

"Blade Merrick." It was a sound of agony across Vittorio's mouth. Still clutching Merrick's throat, Vittorio lifted his head, ordered the men released from the thongs.

Vittorio turned, staring down at Merrick. "Why didn't you speak?" His voice cut at Merrick.

Merrick felt his hands freed, felt the blood return to his wrists and fingers.

He caught Vittorio's hand and tore it loose from his throat.

Vittorio hunkered there. Merrick sat up, still seeing nothing but the fire and blood inside his own head. For a long time Merrick slouched there, head bent.

"You had only to speak," Vittorio said.

Merrick breathed in deeply. His voice was cold. "I beg no one. I beg no Apache for mercy."

"You did not have to beg — only to show this scar, speak your name."

"Did I? Would it have done any good? Did the Apache show my wife any mercy? Would you have shown mercy after your blood brother was killed yesterday?"

"Would you die then, rather than ask for your life?"

Merrick said, "I ask no more than an Apache. Six years ago I was as good as the Apache . . . better. I do not kill women as the Apache kills them."

"Vittorio kills no women."

"Vittorio's people killed my wife. Six years ago. Vittorio's people would have killed me." He raked his hand across the livid scar on his chest. "But the knife of Vittorio's people was not sharp enough to kill me — and the hand of Vittorio's people not strong enough to kill me — only strong enough to rape and kill my wife."

Vittorio stood up. His voice was very low. "Our gods looked down that day six years ago upon injustice. The injustice of the evil among our people attacking the house of the man trying to aid us. Our gods saw rape and murder even as you accuse. This evil still is spoken in the lodges and the wickiups of my people. Apaches among us wronged you by killing your wife and using the knife on you when you had come among us to aid us. That day the chief of all my people asked you to forgive, to remain free to live and hunt and travel our lands among us, never betraying my people, never betrayed by us."

Merrick sagged on the ground. He could not touch his face, the pain was too intense. He could not shut out the memories that raced even more fiery through his mind.

He had gone among the Apaches

during an epidemic that almost wiped them out, working with the Indian agent and army doctors, only to return home to find his house burning and his wife dying after brutal rape. They had tied him up and he had chewed, clawed his way free to fight them to death with his bare hands, to rip out tongues, to claw out eyes, to stop their breathing until they killed him, because he wanted to die, because Mary Beth was dead, but he would not stop fighting them until their knives ripped him open. The savage leader was raking at his guts, Merrick's hand twisting his knife wrist when the tribal leaders overtook the renegades.

Vittorio said, "Vittorio was not at that kill, nor were any of his people. The evil among us had struck at you. Yesterday the bad of your people killed my brother in blood."

Merrick heard the words, but he did not raise his head. The fire in his eyes was making him ill. He wanted to sprawl forward raving on the earth. He wanted to dig out his own eyes.

He remained motionless.

Vittorio said, "Vittorio respects the honorable agreement made between my people and you at the time of your tragedy. You are free now to go among my people — free as you have always been — free forever."

240

# 18

**M**ERRICK pulled himself to his feet. Pain raged through him burning downward from his eyes.

He stood for a moment swaying slightly, legs apart. He saw nothing; the blur before his eyes had not lessened. He shivered, thinking he was blind, to wander helpless the rest of his life in this country, alone and blind.

He moved his head, not attempting to see, but listening. He staggered toward the sound of the water.

He knelt beside the pool, holding his arms across his middle. He was ill.

After a long time he dipped his hands cupped into the water. It was icy against his fevered flesh. He brought the water up to his eyes and forehead as though he could never be cool enough again.

Behind him he heard Vittorio ordering

the Apaches to mount. The young buck who had wanted Valerie lifted his voice in raging protest. Vittorio let him rage a moment, then silenced him with one sharp word. Merrick remained beside the pool on his knees. He did not hear the young brave speak again. As his head cooled he felt again the noon blaze of sun on his back. He heard the slow soft sound of the unshod ponies moving up the incline.

He heard someone beside him. He did not stop bathing his eyes. Dimly, as though through red-darkened glasses saw the ripples of the water surface.

"Blade."

He tensed at the sound of her voice. He remained head bowed over the water.

"Is Jeff all right?" he said.

"I — fixed his bandages. The bleeding has stopped. He is lying beside the wagon."

"All right."

"They've gone. The Indians have gone."

"Yes."

She was silent a moment. He brought the water up against his face.

"They took Clinton's money — that's all they took with them."

"Clinton is lucky."

"Nobody's lucky," she answered. "If it had not been for you, we'd all be dead."

He did not answer. He held the water against his eyes until it spilled through his fingers, or grew warm against his flesh.

"Your wife," Valerie said. "I'm so sorry."

"It was a long time ago."

"Not to you."

"No. Not to me."

"I understand so much now. How you could travel alone through this country with medicine for the missions."

"The army thought I could."

"And you could have — except for us."

"It does not matter."

"It matters. You've been hurt enough . . . too much. I wish there were something I could do."

"There isn't anything."

"They've made you hate," she said. "When they killed your wife, you had nothing left but hate."

"No. It was just that Mary Beth was the only one. I never wanted anyone else."

"Only because you hated everybody."

He opened his mouth to deny this, then closed it. She was speaking the truth. He had lived six years with cold hatred. It was like living forever with ashes in your soul and in your mouth. He had walked through everything, never allowing himself to become part of anything, never seeing anything but the gray shades of the old hate. And then a month ago, the ashes smoldered and the hatred burned again. He saw his brother's stripped body. He hated again, the way he had hated that day when his wife was killed. For this long month, this new hatred had been livid in him. He had lived for one thing, to find the men who had killed his brother and see that they died.

He shuddered, his whole body quivering.

"Blade. Are you all right?"

He did not answer her. He straightened, sitting on his heels. He stared across the cool sump, feeling its coolness, but not seeing anything. He thought about Hardhead Charley Clinton and Perch Fisher and about the way Billy Clinton had died. In his smoky vision he saw the way the Apaches had funneled sand into Perch's nostrils. Perch had tried to save them by not yelling for mercy, even knowing the promise was made in jest. There was a chance that if he did not yell, the tortures might cease; at least the others might die in less than agony. Perch had tried until the sand clogged and scratched his nostril air passages, his throat. Old Clinton had tried, and because he was tougher, he had lasted longer. He had been through hell with them.

He stared at the falling water, sure that he could discern its shape, splashing against the stone at the far wall of the pool. The hatred that had driven him was cooled, only now there was not the taste of ashes, the sense of being dead. He did not want to kill Charley Clinton or Perch Fisher, not even to avenge his brother's death. The horror he'd gone through at Vittorio's hands had purged him of hatred, burned it out of him.

He stood up slowly, vaguely making out the shape of the pool. He would see again, he was sure of it; perhaps existence in the desert had toughened him. He felt only one thing, a need for the woman beside him, something he would never have.

He drew in a deep breath. There was one answer. He had to get out of here, get south to San Carlos. He would be busy there, and she would go her way with her husband, and he would never see her again. At least he had began to live again, had rejoined the human race. She deserved the credit for this, even though he never could have her.

"We better clear out," he said.

She touched his arm. Her fingers dug into his flesh. He turned to face her. He could see her hair only as a bright halo.

She was blurred before him.

Her voice sounded odd, full of tears. "Blade — it won't be the same — for us — after we leave here. We won't see each other again."

His voice was hard. "You'll be all right."

"Yes . . . I'll be all right."

"You take your husband and get back east. You'll be all right."

"I — said I'd be all right." Her voice caught. She said it again, whispering it, protesting. "I'll never see you again."

"We better clear out."

"I never knew anyone like you, Blade. Never even hoped any more I'd find anyone — like you."

His voice was low, desperately savage. "All right. And I want you. Is that what you want to hear? Is that what you need? You think that'll make it any easier?"

"I don't want it to be easier, Blade. I wanted you to know . . . that's all."

Suddenly she was pressed against him. He felt her quivering, crying against his chest. For one last moment he kept his arms at his sides. They came upward almost involuntarily, touching her, his hands hungry, pressing her closer. Her tear-streaked face tilted upward, and he cupped her head in his hand, pressed her mouth against his.

Clinton's voice sounded faraway, then suddenly came close, strong and loud. There was laughter in it, a crazy exultant sound that struck against the walls of the sump.

"That's fine, missy," Clinton shouted from behind Blade. "You just hold what you got. No way we planned it, you couldn't have trapped him better for me."

# 19

**M**ERRICK stepped away from her and turned around. Instinctively he reached for his gun, found his holster empty. He stared toward the place from which Clinton's voice came. He could not see him, but he could hear his wild laughter, coming closer.

"You done fine, missy," Clinton said. He was only a few feet from Merrick now. He was like a dark blur in the bloody world.

"Real good," Perch said, and Merrick could dimly make out his form at Clinton's side.

"How does it feel to be the one without the guns?" Clinton's laughter taunted Merrick. "That Injun left us all our guns. You should have told your ever-loving Injun friend you didn't trust us with firearms."

"He should have known it looking at you."

Valerie stepped around him, pressed close against his side. "You got to believe me, Blade." Her voice was agonized. "I didn't know about this . . . I'd even forgotten what they told me to do."

His voice was cold. "It doesn't matter."

"It's all that matters." She pressed against him, between him and the gunmen. "You've got to believe me."

Clinton laughed. "Tell him you didn't know the Injuns gave us back our guns whilst he was bending over that pool. Tell him you didn't know it. You got him pretty well hooked. He'll believe anything."

Valerie straightened, turning to face them. "I knew. But I thought after all we'd been through . . . he'd saved your lives."

"You thought I'd forget my Billy's death just like that?"

"Yes. You owe him your own life now. We all do."

"Say thank you to the nice man,

Perch," Clinton ordered.

"Thanks," Perch said, voice bitter.

"Now we thanked him, ma'am, you best get out the way. You're right where you could get hurt bad. Now, Perch and me are willing you should ride north with us to Tucson, but we ain't begging you . . . it's just up to you."

Merrick said, "You still think you'll get to Tucson?"

"A lot nearer than you'll ever get again." Clinton stopped langhing, his voice lowered. "You're a brave man, Merrick, I can't deny that, by God — maybe you're even a good man. When all the accounts are in, it's hard to hold everything against you. Looks like you done what you thought you had to — even can see now how you were trying to help us in your way. But I got to have them horses and that wagon."

Valerie said, "You're not going to make it. Those Apaches would like nothing better than to catch you out in that waste country — without Merrick. He's the only one who can get you safely through the Indian country."

"That might have been true. But I'm gambling they'll let his wagon through — if they find out later they been tricked, I can't cry about that. We'll get through. Now if you'll get back yonder to your husband where you belong, we'll clear up this business and get out of here."

Valerie's voice caught in a sob. She turned, pressing against Merrick. "Blade. They'll kill you. There's no way to talk to them. Nothing means anything to them. Tell them you'll turn back — tell them you'll take them to Tucson if they'll let you live."

Merrick exhaled. He closed his arm about her, held her for a moment against him, spoke across her bright hair.

"Why don't you tell her, Clinton? Why don't you tell her the truth, that you couldn't let me live even if I agreed to turn back."

"That's all he wants," Valerie said. She spun around, faced Clinton. "That is all you want. Isn't it?"

Clinton looked at her, his pirate's face twisted. He gave a faint shrug.

"No," Merrick said, voice level. "It wouldn't matter to him even if I agreed to drive them north. It doesn't even matter that he knows he sent Billy out there to kill me and it didn't work out. What he isn't telling you, Valerie, is that if I don't die, he and Perch are lost."

Valerie shivered.

"A month ago," Merrick said, talking to Valerie but staring at the blurred images of Fisher and Clinton, "they robbed a bank in Tucson. I was there. They left town just ahead of me. I had no interest in the bank robbery. I had my brother on my mind. Well, they ran past here on their way to San Carlos. They killed my brother a month ago. Here at Patchee Wells. Now, they've robbed another bank, and even though the Apaches took their loot, they're still guilty of robbery — and murder. There's just one thing they could do — they could let me live to get them past the Injuns and almost to Fort Ambush. But then if they killed me there, they might have to face a murder charge. If they didn't kill me, they'd be sure I'd turn them in at Tucson. So they've got to gamble on the Indians not checking my wagon again. They've got to kill me here and take their chances on the law."

Clinton shrugged.

"And there's more," Merrick said. His voice hardened. "I knew you three had been here before we ever got here."

"Man, you're clever. How'd you figger that?"

"I took a drink from a canteen you had back there in the valley. Billy's canteen. I knew then. His canteen was filled with water from this pool. You killed Ab, but the three of you lied, said you'd never been to this water hole. Because by then the word had caught up with you. You knew the man you killed here was my brother — and you knew I was looking for his killer."

Clinton shrugged. He spoke to Perch. "How about that, Perch? You ever see such a smart fellow?"

"Sin to see him die," Perch said.

Clinton said, "Get out of the way, Mrs. Butler. My temper is short, and it's gettin' late. I'd as soon leave you with him here as not — only you wouldn't enjoy it, because you'd both be dead."

## 20

"CLINTON." Jeff's voice rattled down the incline from the wagon. Merrick raised his head, but could not see Jeff or the wagon. He heard Valerie's sharp intake of breath. She was staring past Clinton and Fisher.

"Don't bother me now, man," Clinton said over his shoulder.

"Clinton. Drop that gun. You, too, Perch."

Clinton turned enough to see Jeff. He had pulled himself to his feet and, propped against the wagon, had staggered around it. He was not able to lift the rifle to his shoulder, but held it at his side, his right hand grasping the trigger.

"Don't make me shoot you, Clinton," Jeff said. "Because I don't want to have to."

Clinton roared. It was the sound of a wounded animal, an outraged pirate, a frustrated Viking yelling against the pound of the North Sea.

"What's the matter with you, Butler?" His voice shook. "You crossing me? I'm the one that'll get you to Tucson. Why you crossing me?"

"Drop your gun, Clinton, and we'll talk about it. I ain't got a lot of patience."

"Look at him." Clinton jerked his head toward Merrick, voice shaking. "He was down here loving up your woman — and you're crossing me for him? The man that's trying to take your wife?"

Butler's voice remained level. "That's my concern, Clinton. I know what I am. I know what he is. The choice between us is up to her."

"Don't be a fool, Butler."

"I'm not a fool. Not any more. I was. But I'm not. I know now what a real man is, what it is to be a man. I never have been one."

"All right, so he's a good man. He's still against everything we want."

"Everything *you* want, Clinton. Merrick has saved my life twice, and as it

257

happens, I hate to be in any man's debt that far."

Perch moved to turn around. Butler said, "Take it easy, Perch. Drop that gun before you turn."

"Jeff. Look out." Valerie screamed.

Clinton stepped wide and swung around, firing as he turned.

The sound of his gun struck against the crack of Jeff's rifle.

Clinton was struck in the chest. He yelled and toppled backward down the incline.

Jeff stayed beside the wagon for a moment, long enough to pull Perch half around to shoot him in case Clinton had missed. But Clinton had not missed. The rifle slipped from Jeff's lifeless fingers. He sagged against the wagon wheel, slid down it and lay still in the sand.

In that moment, Merrick moved. He knew that Jeff had saved his life by shooting Clinton, had given him a chance to stay alive by pulling Perch Fisher around.

Perch was hardly more than a blurred

image before him. Merrick lunged toward him, striking him in the side. He grasped at Perch's right wrist as they hit the ground.

Perch was striking at him. Merrick did not even attempt to protect himself. He battered Perch's gunhand against the rocks, kept hitting until the gun flew from Perch's hand.

Perch got his legs under Merrick and sent him reeling backward.

Perch turned, crouching to dive for his gun. Valerie had run to it, and scooped it up. She turned and ran up the incline. Perch came up off his knees.

Merrick landed on his shoulders, locking his arm under his throat and dragging him off balance. They toppled outward and fell into the pool.

They went under, kicking and thrashing.

Merrick fought his way upward. Fisher was beating at his head as he surfaced. He caught Fisher about the middle and dragged him under. His lungs felt as if they would burst. He put his foot in Perch's stomach and thrust downward.

His head cleared the surface and he gasped for air. Perch caught him and pulled him under.

By now Perch was fighting for the surface. Merrick caught him by the throat and pulled him back. Perch fought frantically, his mouth opening, and he swallowed water.

Merrick managed to get his own head above the water without loosening his grasp on Fisher's throat. His fingers tightened and he pressed down. Fisher caught at his hands, pulling, but his fingers were already weakening, and then he was not fighting any more.

Merrick lunged away from him, pulled himself up on the rocks. He sat there for a long time, staring at the body in the pool.

A shiver wracked through him.

He caught Perch Fisher by the shirt collar and pulled him from the water.

Valerie came slowly down the incline. Her eyes were brimming with tears, but her head was tilted.

"Jeff," she said. "Jeff is dead."

But she said it with a sense of pride and a sense of loss. Merrick thought that no matter how low Jeff had sunk in her estimation, he had redeemed himself with her and he hadn't died in vain.

Merrick worked in the sun with the spade. The sun blared, sinking slowly. The coppery sky was reflected in the pool. It was late afternoon before the three men were buried.

Valerie sat beside the wells and waited for him. The darkness was settling when he tossed the spade into the wagon.

She got up and came to him.

"We better head out," he said. "We can be in San Carlos in the morning."

"Yes, Blade," she said. "I'm ready to go."

He touched her hand. Her fingers enclosed his. They walked up the incline. He helped her into the wagon, climbed to the seat beside her. He glanced at the graves down the incline from the wells, gazed once more at the cool sump. He spoke to the horses, slapped the reins across them.

The wagon moved slowly up the incline, crested the run and headed south.

Valerie did not look back again.

It was a long time before the wagon was out of sight of the water hole. Darkness came slowly, fading in from the mountains where the haze was purple, rolling in across the flat wastes. The wind came up, and it covered the heel prints in the sand, and blew the earth across the wagon tracks so there was no trace of them. The stillness settled with the night. White men had come here to Patchee Wells — and Indians. For a little while, the silence had been broken. But the white men passed, and the Indians; the silence settled again, breathless and unbroken.

The water hole was as it was before, as it was in the beginning, and forever.